TALES OF
Don Quixote
BOOK II

TALES OF
Don Quixote

BOOK II

RETOLD BY BARBARA NICHOL

Tundra Books

Published in Canada by Tundra Books,
75 Sherbourne Street, Toronto, Ontario M5A 2P9

Published in the United States by Tundra Books of Northern New York,
P.O. Box 1030, Plattsburgh, New York 12901

Library of Congress Control Number: 2005910638

Library and Archives Canada Cataloguing in Publication

Nichol, Barbara (Barbara Susan Lang)
    Tales of Don Quixote : book II / retold by Barbara Nichol.

ISBN-13: 978-0-88776-744-9
ISBN-10: 0-88776-744-3

    1. Don Quixote (Fictitious character)–Juvenile fiction. 2. Spain–
Juvenile fiction. 3. Knights and knighthood–Juvenile fiction. 4. Quests
(Expeditions)–Juvenile fiction. I. Cervantes Saavedra, Miguel
de, 1547-1616. Don Quixote.Title. II. Title.

PS8577.I165T342 2006   jC813'.54   C2005-907310-1

ONTARIO ARTS COUNCIL
CONSEIL DES ARTS DE L'ONTARIO

We acknowledge the financial support of the Government of Canada through the
Book Publishing Industry Development Program (BPIDP)
and that of the Government of Ontario through the Ontario Media
Development Corporation's Ontario Book Initiative. We further acknowledge the
support of the Canada Council for the Arts and the Ontario Arts Council for our
publishing program.

Design: Cindy Elisabeth Reichle
Printed and bound in Canada

This book is printed on acid-free paper that is100% recycled,
ancient-forest friendly (40% post-consumer recycled).

1 2 3 4 5 6   11 10 09 08 07 06

i carry your heart with me(i carry it in
my heart)
– ee cummings

Acknowledgments

I started this book after making a radio documentary on *Don Quixote* for CBC Radio's "Ideas" series. The shows involved almost two years of interviews and conversations with scholars whose names will be very familiar to anyone who has studied Cervantes. They are: A.J. Close, Barry Ife, Diana de Armas Wilson, Carroll B. Johnson, James Iffland, James Parr, Donald McCrory, Burton Raffel, Daniel Eisenberg, Eduardo Urbina, Edward H. Friedman, and Maria Antonia Garcés. I am so grateful for their time and insights.

I read a number of translations and editions of *Don Quixote* in preparing to write this: among them, the very highly regarded new translations by Burton Raffel, John Rutherford, and Edith Grossman, and the classic translations by Tobias Smollett, Walter Starkie, Charles Jarvis, and John Ormsby.

Many thanks to Bernie Lucht at CBC Radio, to Barry Moser, and to Kong Njo, Kathryn Cole, and – once again – Kathy Lowinger at Tundra Books.

PROLOGUE

I will keep this prologue short: just some things to keep in mind and catch you up before you read.

Four hundred years ago, a man named Miguel de Cervantes wrote the work the book you hold is based on. His book was called *The Ingenious Gentleman Don Quixote de La Mancha.* Some people say this was the world's first novel. The book found brand-new ways to say and show things – new ways to say what the author thought and felt, and how he saw the world.

In fact, Miguel de Cervantes was so ingenious himself that after all these centuries, other authors are still trying to catch up.

This is Book II of my retelling of his story: the conclusion of my version of Cervantes' book.

Tales of Don Quixote (Book I), if you missed it, told the first part of the story of an ordinary gentleman who somehow came to think he was a knight.

He was an *hidalgo*: a sort of Spanish gentleman who lived four hundred years ago. He was the sort of gentleman that histories don't trouble to make note of. He had a little money. He tended a small estate that had been passed down to him through family. He lived there with his housekeeper and niece. He owned one horse and a single dog (a greyhound). The highlight of his week was Sunday dinner. On Sundays he ate pigeon for a treat.

For many of us this would be enough. But Don Quixote had a questing soul. As he grew old, as time ahead grew short, he saw his modest, quiet life stretching out behind him and before him. What, when all was said and done, would such an uneventful life add up to? There came upon Quixote the restlessness that's often born of longing. And then a day he could no longer bear it.

Furthermore, Don Quixote's brain dried up from reading. So says the book on which this book is based. Our hero lost his mind from reading books.

He read books of adventure – dragons slain and damsels saved. He read the books of chivalry. Perhaps for years these books were thrill enough. But, as I say, there came a day when Don Quixote's thinking took a turn. He came to believe the stories in the books he read were true, and that he was a brave and famous knight.

He conjured up a knightly name: Quixote. He went into the world to seek adventure and took a peasant neighbor as his squire.

As Book I reached its finish, Quixote and his squire, a fat and friendly type named Sancho Panza, were brought home from their strange and comic foray – brought home by their worried friends, to the great relief of all who knew them. Don Quixote, who was old and ill and tired, was brought home in a cage upon an oxcart.

I guess this will be obvious: their quests had not turned out as they had hoped.

⟨⟨⟨⟩⟩⟩

When Miguel de Cervantes' book was published, it was a great success. Suddenly its author, who had spent his life in poverty and hardship, was famous. For the record, he never became rich.

He published his Book II some ten years later.

But in literary life, as elsewhere, there are snakes who lie among the weeds.

Before Cervantes had a chance to write his second book, another author beat him to the punch. Another author used Cervantes' characters to write a book that was – he claimed – the further stories of the great Quixote. He stole Cervantes' characters. And if this weren't sin enough, in the introduction to his book, he ridiculed Cervantes in the cruelest terms. He called Cervantes old. (He was almost sixty when Book I was published.) He mocked Cervantes for his crippled hand. (Cervantes had been injured in a war, fighting bravely in a naval battle.)

At the publication of the false Book II, Cervantes was, quite properly, enraged.

Enough for now. There will be opportunities (galore) to dwell upon the evils of the false Book II.

꘎꘎꘎

As I say, Book I of Don Quixote was very popular. It was under every nose, before each pair of spectacles in Spain.

But there were some criticisms, too. Cervantes sometimes lost track of the details. He called Sancho's wife by different names in different places in the book. There were other little things like this.

In Book II – the *real* Book II – Cervantes has his characters discuss this. Sancho says it was the printer's fault.

The book was also criticized for slowing down for stories that didn't have to do with Don Quixote: stories, for example, that another character might tell.

In bringing you Book I, I left these stories out and

stayed with Don Quixote, start to finish. I've done this in Book II as well. I've left out stories Don Quixote overhears and those that don't concern his fortunes as a knight.

ᏣᎳᎯ

A final word: In Spain, when Miguel de Cervantes wrote his book, religion was dictated by the state. It was legal only to be Christian. It was against the law to be a Jew. It was against the law to be a Muslim.

The Muslims in this book are Turks or Moors. Spaniards sometimes said that Moors were liars.

They say it in this book from time to time.

Did Cervantes think that Moors were liars? Consider this.

Cervantes tells us that he did not invent the tale of Don Quixote. He says the story comes from a translation of a version of events collected from old documents, pieced together by a Moor. His name was Benengeli. Don Quixote tells us all along that Benengeli's version of his life is the only one that can be trusted. The Moor named Benengeli tells the truth.

And by the way, is all of this confusing? Don't try too hard to keep the whole thing straight. The great Miguel de Cervantes is showing us a world – the real world as it really is – in which we often can't be sure which end is up.

Where were we?

It is four hundred years ago.

Cervantes lifts his pen. Don Quixote, in his bed at home, blinks his weary eyes. He moves his skinny legs beneath the covers. He clears his throat. He lifts his spoon and takes a tiny sip of healing broth.

Book II of Don Quixote – the real Book II – begins.

If there are errors, they're the printer's fault.

The Knight is Recovered;
Visitors Arrive; "There is a Book!"

⬥⬥⬥

Some weeks had passed since Don Quixote had come home, brought back to his village by his friends, brought low by his adventures on the road. Tall and getting on in years and much too thin, he'd seemed about to die when he'd returned, yellow with disease yet clinging to delusions with an iron strength.

Twice he'd sallied forth into the world to do good deeds – sallied; that's what they used to say. Once he'd gone alone, and once with Sancho Panza, the simple local peasant he'd appointed squire. Sancho, whose simplicity (by which I mean he wasn't very clever) made him a believing ear for all his master's cockamamie plans. Sancho, whose shortness and whose fleshiness, whose roly-poly ballast and whose bloat (which means that he was fat) made such a striking contrast to Don Quixote's tall, enfeebled frame.

⬥⬥⬥

While Quixote lay in bed these weeks, his friends, the priest and barber, paid visits to the women of Quixote's house. They came for tidings of the patient's health, and bade the housekeeper and niece to tend him carefully. Of course, the women needed no such guidance. His housekeeper and niece, they loved Quixote dearly. They washed his limbs and combed his hair and wrapped him up to keep him warm. They listened to his whisperings and ravings, praying that his madness would subside. And there was cause for hope. In the quiet of his room, Quixote's talk of knighthood did die down.

And so it was, that one fine day, the priest and barber decided it was time to pay a visit to Quixote's bedside. The housekeeper and niece brought them in.

There was Don Quixote in his bed, still wizened and still withered. At the very best of times Quixote had been only skin and bones. This day, despite a crimson cap and vest, he called to mind a wrapped Egyptian mummy. Even so, he sat up in his bed to greet his friends and was alert and sensible and seemed to be brought round by manly company.

The priest and barber had made a pact before they paid their call, to stay away from subjects that might inflame Quixote's knightly dreams. And so, the men beside the bed talked of great events, but nothing that would strike too close to home. They spoke about affairs of state, about the proper conduct of a government. They chewed on great ideas: this and that. And there was news! It seemed the Turks (the Moors with whom the Spanish had bad blood) were threatening – God defend us! – to invade. There was a mighty fleet approaching Spain. What was the king to do?

Well, Don Quixote had a simple answer.

"I would recommend a course of action I'm sure His Majesty has not considered: the easiest, most reasonable of plans."

The priest and barber scoffed at Don Quixote. The king was surely offered plans from dawn to dusk.

"What plan?" they asked. "What is this strategy the king himself will not have heard?"

"I will not share it, lest the king should hear it from another source and the credit does not fall to me."

Quixote's friends assured him that they would not divulge his secret plan.

"The king," said Don Quixote "should send a public crier out to every part of Spain to call in all knights. Together they will fight the evil Turk."

All the knights in Spain? Was Quixote still insisting that the stories in the storybooks were true?

The sickly hero upon the bed continued. "In fact, a proper knight could do the job alone. There are knights who have been known to chop up armies – two thousand men – as though they had one throat to cut between them, as if they had been made of sugar candy."

A knight. He spoke of knights. The priest and barber caught each other's eye.

The subject had been raised despite their caution.

"Oh dear," exclaimed the niece. "Oh, strike me dead! Our master still believes he is a knight."

The figure in the bed turned red with rage.

"I am and always will be," roared the invalid – the living mummy in the crimson cap.

Oh dear!

He thinks he is a knight.

Silence stuffed its way into the room.

"I am a knight," Quixote shook with anger, "who only seeks to show the world how foolish it has been. The world has turned its back on virtues of an age gone by. Knights were once great men. They did not always spend their days, as they do now, indulging in the comforts of the court. They gave their hours over to the highest ends: protecting damsels, coming to the aid of helpless orphans, admonishing the proud, and raising up the humble from their sorrows."

Silence once again within the sickroom.

The ladies drifted off and down the hall. The barber and the priest stayed on a while, raising other topics by and by. They talked about the size of different giants. They talked of famous ladies and their virtues. And then, of ladies and their famous vices.

The heavy weather was becalmed for now. In the sick-room shouts gave way to murmurs. But wind was picking up on the horizon. A wind you'll recognize as Sancho Panza – the peasant who had been Quixote's squire.

For Sancho Panza also chose this day to pay a call. Coincidence. And there were loud objections from the ladies.

Don Quixote and the priest and barber listened from within Quixote's room.

"You will not come inside," the ladies roared. "It is your fault our master's lost his senses. It is your fault he almost lost his life. Have you come back to lead our poor misguided master off anew, to lead him over hill and dale to danger?"

"It's he who led *me* into danger," said the squire. "He told me our adventures would end up in my being made a king, or governing an island all my own." (And this was so. Quixote had made promises like these. He made them and had certainly believed them.)

In Quixote's bedroom, the priest and barber took their hats from off the bed and, gesturing farewells, brought their visit to a quiet close. But Don Quixote, hearing Sancho's voice, cried out. He bade the women hold their tongues and bring his faithful squire to his room.

And so the two – Don Quixote and his Sancho Panza, noble knight and dim but loyal friend – were at last brought face-to-face again. What great events the two had shared: the onslaught on the windmills that Don Quixote had believed were giants, the fight with sheep the knight had thought were armies, the fearless feat of setting free the chain gang that Don Quixote wrongly took for innocents, the rescue of the maiden Quixote had mistaken for a princess, mistaking also that she had been kidnapped.

Memories came crowding round the bed, demanding notice from the two, jostling and whispering, jockeying for space and for position.

It had been some weeks since their adventures. Their lives had been unspotted by events. Don Quixote had been confined to bed. Sancho Panza had been herding goats.

But as it does, the world had kept on spinning, and Sancho had some stunning news to tell.

There was a book!

The Ingenious Gentleman Don Quixote of La Mancha it was called. And in it were the tales of their adventures.

A book! Don Quixote's mind began to tilt. How could this be? Most of their great exploits had taken place when no one else was present. What author could have known of these events? And how could he have known of them so soon?

Don Quixote turned this question over in his muddled mind – looked at it from one side and the other. How is the inexplicable explained?

Well, those of us who know the knight will guess what sort of answer he came up with. Enchanters. Enchanters must have followed them and taken notes.

"And who," Quixote asked the squire, "was given credit as the story's author?"

"Cide Hamete Benengeli," said Sancho. "A Moor."

"A Moor!" said Don Quixote. "A Turk? This must mean the story of our sallies was written in a language we don't know."

"Yes," said Sancho Panza, "and rendered into Spanish by another hand. And now the book is read in several countries. The truth is, Master, you and I are famous!"

Now Sancho did not move in bookish circles. (He hobnobbed with the set that herded goats.) In fact, he'd only heard this news the night before. A student who was called Sanson Carrasco had come home from his studies in a distant town. He was a graduate – a Bachelor of Learning – and he had brought the news back to La Mancha.

Don Quixote, burning with excitement, his red cap like a flame upon his head, wished to meet this student right away.

The Bachelor: The Third Sally Begins; The Trip to El Toboso.

⁂

S anson Carrasco – Bachelor of Learning – was produced at Don Quixote's bedside. He had the sort of face, the story says, that made it plain he had a jesting spirit: round in shape, large of mouth, and flat of nose. He was witty. He was twenty-four years old.

Though the news about the book had greatly lifted Don Quixote's spirits, the knight had some concerns about its contents. Did the book describe Quixote's greatness? And did it represent his faithful heart; his devotion to his Lady Fair, the perfect and the peerless Dulcinea? Did it capture properly her splendor and the many times the knight had spurned romances in her name? Was the book, in short, the truthful tale? After all, it had been written by a Moor. Moors, as Don Quixote knew, were not to be depended on for truth. (He knew this for a fact, as he knew that horses sometimes fly, that knights who had been cut in half could be stuck back together, right as rain, and that there are great kingdoms underwater.)

⚭

On all accounts the Bachelor Carrasco had nothing but good news to tell the knight. It was a book to make its heroes proud.

"And will there be a sequel?" asked Quixote.

"They say," explained Carrasco, "that even now the author's looking high and low for further tales. So far he has had no luck at all."

"Well then," said Sancho Panza to Quixote, "you must get out of bed. We must provide this Moor with more to tell."

And thus the matter set itself before them. The briskly spinning world, it seems, awaited. Don Quixote wondered if he had the strength for one more sally. Would events conspire in his favor?

And then from just beyond the walls of his small house, he heard a sound that answered all his doubts. It was the neighing of his horse – his trusty shopworn steed, his Rocinante.

Quixote knew an omen when he heard one. The horse had neighed. The time had come. Quixote would go back into the world.

⚭

Though he did his best to keep this secret, the women of the house would not be fooled. In the days that followed, the household was the site of tears and strife – a battleground of views that clashed and sentiments that met in opposition. The housekeeper was fretful beyond telling. She visited the Bachelor Carrasco, begging him to change her master's mind.

"My master was half dead when he came home. It took six hundred eggs to make him well. And if you don't believe me ask my hens. You know that hens will only tell the truth."

The student was not moved by honest hens.

Quixote's niece was terrified as well, and tried her best to change her uncle's mind. She did not mince words. "You are old," she said to Don Quixote, "and stupid if you think you're young." (Tact was not an arrow in her quiver.) "You're ill, although you think that you are well. You think you are a knight, but you're mistaken."

Alas, she made her arguments for nothing.

As for Sancho Panza, he had some business details to discuss.

You will recall that on their first adventures, Sancho had been confident that he would be made an earl or count or king. It was a squire's due instead of payment.

Though Sancho was not endlessly observant, he'd noticed he had not become a monarch. His only subjects were, as they had been for years, his wife, a son, a daughter, and an ass (whose name was Dapple), along with other sundry barnyard types.

So Sancho paid a visit to Quixote and asked if, this time out, he might be paid.

"My blabbermouthed and feebleminded friend," Quixote came directly to the point. "Nowhere in the history of knights and squires are there squires who take their money by the week. Squires must show faith that they will share in the avails of victories. I will never be the knight who topples this tradition on its head. Feel free to stay at home. Spend your lifetime sieving wheat and slopping pigs. There are other squires who would serve me."

And just as Don Quixote had predicted, a would-be squire did indeed appear. It was the round-faced, flat-nosed, large-mouthed Bachelor Carrasco, arriving in a merry, troublemaking mood.

"Oh, flower of knight-errantry," he said. "Nothing must delay you from your quests. Nothing must cast gloom across your path. Oh, honor of all Spain, it would be my privilege to serve you."

The wings of Sancho Panza's heart drooped. (So says the book.) His eyes filled up with tears. It had not even crossed his mind that Don Quixote would take some other person as his squire.

"It is my wife," said Sancho, "who put me up to making these demands."

He would be Quixote's squire again, and wait for his reward as squires must.

⁂

Quixote found a helmet – sturdy, if adorned with dust and mold. Sancho Panza loaded up his ass with food and drink.

The women wrung their hands and wept. They clawed their faces, tore their clothes, and mourned. But Don Quixote would not be deterred.

By light of moon, Don Quixote mounted Rocinante. Sancho Panza found a spot to perch among the bags of food on Dapple's back.

Thus, knight and squire were on their way. The Bachelor Carrasco rode with the adventurers to see them off. He rode with them a little while and then turned back, returning to the village in the dark.

They ventured forth – Quixote and his squire, Sancho Panza – two moonstruck souls in search of new adventures, enough, they hoped, to fill another book.

⁂

A knight must have a Lady Fair – a lady whom he loves beyond distraction. It's in her name a knight performs his feats. Often she's the daughter of a king. This creature must be beautiful and clever: the purpose of her life is to delight. Her hands are only suitable for stitchery and stringing pearls. Her voice is only raised in tinkling song. Frail she is, and delicate and sheltered from the shuntings of the world.

Now as you know, Don Quixote had a Lady Fair, although we must admit she was, to some extent, a figment of his own imagination. (Quixote was ingenious, it's true.) Knowing that such ladies are so very rare (suspecting, I'm afraid, they don't exist), he'd chosen from the local girls a favorite and invested all his fantasies in her. Indeed, this act took leaps of ingenuity. He'd only seen this girl perhaps four times.

Though comely, this peasant girl wasn't what story-books described. She was large and she was raw boned – a sunburned sweaty sort, handsome, if this type is to your taste. Did she stitch and string together pearls? If she did, the story does not tell it. Did she raise her voice in tinkling song? Indeed, she raised her voice, but not in song. She could holler loud enough, the locals said, to summon far-flung workers home for meals. And was she frail and sheltered? She worked long days and rollicked in the rough-and-tumble world of working men.

But Quixote kept these details in their place. As anyone who's been in love will know, we can ignore whatever attributes we wish our lover did not have (they vanish!), and conjure up the ones that we'd prefer. Love is enchantment and we are the magicians, however much the spell we cast might fade.

He called her by a name that he'd invented: Dulcinea del Toboso. Did she even know that he existed? Perhaps she did. Most likely she did not.

And did our knight believe in Dulcinea – in this sweet concoction of his troubled mind? Perhaps he did – or wished he did so earnestly that it was just as if he did. Or didn't, but pretended that he did. This is for you, dear Reader, to decide.

⁂

In any case, the first step on this sally would be to pay a visit to the Lady Fair to ask her for her blessing on the venture. From there the pair would leave for Saragossa for the jousting. The knight would win a contest in her name.

This was their plan, but there were complications. Quixote did not know where Dulcinea lived. Certainly she lived in El Toboso. (He'd embedded her location in her name.) But where exactly was the lady's palace?

Now, if you've read the first book, you'll know Quixote'd once sent Sancho off to find her. He'd sent him with a letter to deliver. But Sancho had not found her, you'll recall. In fact, he had not gone to El Toboso. Instead, he'd done the next best thing. He'd pretended to Quixote that he'd found her, and Don Quixote'd never been the wiser.

That first day the two rode to El Toboso, and reached its outskirts as the day grew dim. How would they find the lady? Don Quixote had an inspiration. What they should do, and right away, was wait. Why should they wait? We are not told, but wait they did 'til midnight, outside town.

And then, by dark of night, to the intermittent calling of the alley cats, and to the barking of the dogs behind the gates and, from time to time, to the gruntings of the sleeping pigs, they rode into the town of El Toboso.

"You've been here before," Quixote said to Sancho. "Now take me to the palace where you found her."

"Perhaps it's down this alley," Sancho said, groping to conceal that he had lied. "I think it's down this alley that I found her."

"There are no palaces in alleys," said the knight. Dogs barked and cats meowed and slithered past.

"The truth is, as I once explained," the squire said, "she wasn't in a palace when I saw her, but outside in a yard and sieving wheat. I don't remember where it was exactly."

"You are, of course, mistaken," said the knight. "Ladies Fair do not spend time in yards. Think carefully, and we will find her palace."

"Well, if it was a palace," said the squire, "you must have seen this palace for yourself. She is your Lady Fair, not mine. Where is her palace? You must know it better than I."

"Not so," said Don Quixote. "I need not have laid eyes on her to love her. I need not have encountered her at all. I love her based on nothing more than legend — on the stories of her wit and beauty."

It was a stalemate in the empty streets. At dawn they stopped a farmhand who was leaving to begin a day of work. He had never heard of Dulcinea. He scratched his head and looked down at the ground. He did not think the town had much to offer in the way of Ladies Fair.

The sun came up. The time had come for rooster calls and stirring pigs, and soon, the fuss and bother of the human beasts.

And dawned as well, in Sancho Panza's worried brain, a strategy to buy a little time. Quixote should take shelter in a grove of trees outside the town. Sancho would go forth and find the Lady.

(Oh, more than once, within this tale we find our Sancho Panza more clever than the Sancho of Book I. The Sancho of this second book is often not the simple-minded peasant of the first.)

Sancho left his master in a nearby wood and walked a little way toward the town. He found a place to sit and sort his thoughts. He knew there was no Lady Dulcinea. At least he did suspect that this was so. How, then, could he produce her for Quixote?

Sancho Panza's thoughts began to drift, to roam and wander off to other matters. How had he ended up in such a fix? He asked himself the question thus: "My master is a lunatic. What must I be to leave my home and join him?"

A lunatic. A lunatic! This word it seems, suggested a solution. His master was a lunatic. He took windmills for giants. He once mistook a flock of sheep for armies. So Sancho did not need to find Fair Dulcinea. He needed only find a girl and say that it was she. Quixote's ingenuity would fill the gap.

And as the squire's scheme emerged, there too emerged three peasant girls on donkeys, coming straight toward him from the town.

Three Peasant Girls;
The Knight of The Forest

I will not lie. These were not the sort of girls that make the poets lift their pens and minstrels sing. Fat of arm they were, and low of brow. But girls they were, and coming right his way.

Sancho found his feet. He pitched himself upon his grazing ass. He must make haste. He had good news to take to Don Quixote. Here was Dulcinea with her servants!

Sancho found the knight as he had left him – upon his horse, his feet in stirrups, leaning on his lance; at ease but ever ready to do battle.

"Dulcinea del Toboso is approaching." said the squire. "And with her are two servants. All three are so magnificent it's like they travel in a golden cloud. They wear brocade, ten layers thick, and all three are bedecked in precious gems. Their tresses flow in waves of shifting light. Come, Master! Your Lady Fair approaches. Waste no time!"

And so, Quixote rode out from the shady wood. At last he would lay eyes upon the lady of his thoughts. He spurred his horse. He fixed his gaze. He peered. But who was this approaching up the road? Three wenches on three dusty, trudging beasts. (Three dusty, trudging beasts approached on donkeys.)

"I don't see Dulcinea here," he said. Sancho must have seen three other maidens. "These are, instead, three peasant girls."

"Dear Master, have you lost your sight?" the squire asked, sputtering with made-up disbelief. "Are your eyes on backwards? Do you not see Lady Dulcinea, shining up ahead just like the sun?"

Once the girls were close at hand, Sancho climbed down from his ass's back. He took one of their donkeys by the halter. He chose a moon-faced, snub-nosed girl to be his master's Lady Dulcinea.

"Oh, queen and princess, duchess of great beauty," said the squire to the moon-faced girl. "Paragon of all that is most fine and good, I show to you your hapless knight, Quixote. He's tongue-tied in the presence of your greatness. Even so, he is your loyal servant, the Knight of Mournful Countenance. And I, his loyal squire, Sancho Panza."

Now these three girls were peasants on their way to many hours of labor – a day more taxing than our heroes faced. They did not wish their long day made yet longer, not by silly seeming men, talking nonsense, wearing fancy dress. And so we will forgive their rough replies.

"Out of the way!" said one. "I'll currycomb you like my father's she-ass."

Was this perplexing threat the sort of thing that Lady Dulcinea's servant would deliver? Why was she not compliant and refined? Could Don Quixote really be convinced that this was Dulcinea and her servants?

Just as Sancho Panza had predicted, Don Quixote's fantasies were equal to the challenge of the moment. He could make the puzzle pieces fit. With reeling brain and clouded eyes, Don Quixote looked upon the snub-nosed girl and let his wishful brain perform its magic. Yes! Possibly this was his Dulcinea. He squinted and he strained to make it so. He bore down on the project of believing until the pieces fell into their proper place.

Suddenly, the knight was certain. Yes. It was so. This was his Lady Fair, disguised. Some enchanter or magician had cast a spell to alter her appearance to rob from him the sight of her magnificence.

"Oh, perfection of all excellence the heart desires." He said this to the snub-nosed peasant girl. "Oh, soul of human courtesy. You are the only balm that cures my troubled heart – the heart that beats for you alone. A sorcerer has seen to it, alas, that your beauty has been debased and put askew, so that I see before me nothing but a plain and filthy peasant.

This is how enchanters do torment me. Have they made me horrible as well? I beg you not to turn away. Do not refuse to look on me with love."

"Hey, Granddad. Move aside," said "Dulcinea." (In fairness, she was not exactly flattered.)

With that she struck her donkey with a stick. She would escape and get on with her day. The donkey, though, did not expect a beating. He jumped ahead and threw her to the ground. Quixote rushed to help the lady to her feet. She shook him off. She backed up several steps and took a run toward her ass and hiking up her ragged skirts, leapfrogged from behind to board the beast. And she was off – she and her companions, beating a retreat along the road.

How cruel were the magicians. They stole from Don Quixote the vision he'd for so long longed to see. And, by the way, enchanters had not been content at hiding Dulcinea's glowing beauty. There was another change they wrought, which honesty compels me to record. How can I put this prettily, dear Reader? Perhaps I'll leave it out. No. I will not. Children should be told the truth.

She stank.

⟜∞⟝

Their mission thus accomplished, Don Quixote and his squire started on the road to Saragossa, for Saragossa was, each year, the setting for a contest known as jousting.

Jousting (which has now slipped out of fashion) is a fight between two men on horseback. They charge straight at each other, lances raised and pointed forth. The object is to knock the other off his horse. (I say "men" when I refer to the contestants. Women do not settle scores on horseback.)

To get back to our heroes, though, they found a peaceful spot to pass the night – a clump of trees to shelter and protect them. Sancho Panza settled down beneath an oak, the knight beneath a cork tree quite close by. Rocinante and the ass took up the positions they reverted to whenever there were lulls between adventures.

Bear with me please, dear Reader. I'll interrupt the story for a moment. The fellow who translated from the Arabic has something he would like to have us know. He tells us that the Moor called Benengeli carries on for page on page about the love that grew between the animals – Sancho Panza's ass and Rocinante. He tells us he, the translator, has left out several chapters on this subject, for reasons of decorum and for length.

But there is one detail he'll pass on, and that is that the beasts had come up with a way of resting all their own. The horse would drop his neck over the donkey's neck. Then both would bend their heads, looking down toward the ground, one head resting gently on the other. Embracing thus, they'd stay this way for days.

⟋⟍⟋⟍⟍⟍

Quixote slept. Sancho slept.

Two men on horseback rode into the wood and stopped to make their camp nearby.

Don Quixote woke to creaks of armor.

"We'll stop here," said an unfamiliar voice. Don Quixote listened in the dark. "There's grass here for the horses and all the solitude I need to dwell upon my tragic tale of love."

Don Quixote listened with his keenest ear. This stranger knew the dreadful woes of love? This stranger had to be a kindred spirit. Chances were the stranger was a knight. Quixote sensed adventure in the offing. He woke up Sancho Panza with a whisper.

As Don Quixote and his squire listened, lying still as stones upon the ground, the lovesick knight embarked upon a song. He sang about his helplessness, his broken heart. He sang and then he stopped his song to speak.

"Most beautiful, ungrateful one," he said, lamenting to a lover who was absent. "How can it be that you allow your luckless knight to waste away his life in endless missions? Is it not enough that you are acknowledged far and wide as most perfect of all women in your beauty – proclaimed so by the knights in Navarre, in Leon and Andalusia and in Castile and even by the famous Don Quixote?"

Quixote? The stranger in the dark spoke of Quixote? Quixote heard his name and was confused. This stranger claimed that he had forced Quixote to deem some other Lady Fair most lovely? More lovely than the Lady Dulcinea?

Now, once there was a time when Don Quixote would have been so thoroughly provoked by what he'd heard, he would have let the stranger taste his sword. But on this night our hero felt a rush of tenderness toward his fellow knight – this brokenhearted swain upon the ground.

"He is deluded, Sancho," said Quixote. "Let's listen. I am certain more will be revealed."

"Have no fear that more will be revealed," said Sancho, still half asleep and, wishing he were wholly so, not inclined to keep his voice a whisper. "I fear this knight might carry on his whimpering for weeks."

"Who goes there?" asked the grieving knight. He'd heard them.

And thus the knights were introduced. The stranger knight was called Knight of The Forest. We will call his squire the Forest Squire.

Knowing that his bleatings had been overheard, the knight had questions for Quixote. "Are you in love as well?"

"Of course," said Don Quixote. "I'm a knight."

"And does your Lady Fair disdain you?" asked the other.

"I have never been disdained," Quixote said. (This despite the girl who'd called him Granddad.)

"My master's lady is a gentle lamb," said Sancho, "and softer than a pat of yellow butter."

The Forest Knight cast narrowed eyes on Sancho. "And does your squire pipe up anytime he likes? Does he always talk without permission?"

The squire of the Forest Knight took hold of Sancho's arm and led him off. They would retreat to someplace close where they could talk and not disturb their masters.

Indeed, alone, with no one to restrain them, the squires found that they had much in common. Both would be rewarded with positions for their years as squires: Sancho would be ruler of an island. The Forest Squire confided that he would have some lofty role within the church. They discovered, also, that their masters were alike in certain ways. Both knights were brave and both a bit befuddled. Both, in fact, were probably insane.

"I take comfort," said our Sancho, "that your master is as cockeyed as my own. But let me add that Don Quixote's pure of heart. He hasn't any drop of malice in him. Because of this I can't seem to abandon him, howevermuch ridiculous he is. I love him. That's the honest truth. God help me."

On this ringing note of frank emotion, the Squire of the Forest brought out from his saddlebag a rabbit pie and even better, a wineskin, full to bursting.

"I love this wineskin so" he said to Sancho. "I smother it with kisses all day long." Yes! Squires, too, can give their hearts away. And Sancho, he was likewise a romantic. Sancho's love for wineskins knew no bounds.

Both squires' eyes grew watery with feeling for the sloshing object of their hearts. They drank the wine and ate the pie until their eyes rolled back into their heads. They fell asleep, their passion spent, their dinners still half-chewed within their mouths.

The knights' encounter was, of course, more dignified, as the lovelorn Forest Knight told the story of his broken heart.

It seems his Lady Fair was most demanding. His lady would not easily be won. She would set one mission, and then another. And when each task was finished, she'd set the fellow yet another goal.

He'd conquered La Giralda the Giantess. She was a figure spinning on a steeple – a famous monster made of brass. In his lady's name, he made her still. He'd lifted up four ancient stones. They were called the Bulls of Guisando. His Lady Fair commanded him to lift them. He did so – a task that took great toil. And on another mission, he'd thrown himself into a yawning cavern because she wished to know what lay inside.

Finally, she'd sent him on a journey to visit all the provinces of Spain, to win from every other knight the admission that she was, of all the ladies in the world, most beautiful. And this he'd almost done, he said. His proudest feat was winning this concession from Quixote.

"I do not think you conquered Don Quixote," answered Don Quixote. "Perhaps it was another knight who looked like him."

"Oh, it was he. A very tall and skinny man, his face a nest of wrinkles, with beakish nose and drooping black moustache."

"I tell you," said Quixote, "the description might be accurate, but you are wrong. I can tell you this because Quixote is my friend. We are so close, if truth be told, it's almost as if I am he myself. It seems to me some sort of magic is afoot. And this would not surprise me. Quixote is tormented by enchanters. And I can tell you this, for I am he. I am Don Quixote, who will defend my lady's name in combat."

And thus did Don Quixote challenge the sad stranger to a joust.

The Forest Knight agreed to fight Quixote, but told our hero this: "Our battle must take place at dawn. We will not fight by dark of night as highwaymen and bullies do. Furthermore, I ask for one condition. Whomever is knocked from his horse will be at the disposal of the victor, to do whatever he might ask, provided that whatever thing it is, is proper and becoming for a knight."

It was agreed. The two went off to find their squires, to let them know a joust was in the offing. They woke the squires, told them of the plan, and then retreated.

∽

According to the Forest Squire, there was a custom in his land that Sancho Panza did not know existed: when knights do battle, squires fight as well.

"While our masters fight, we'll take up clubs and beat each other senseless."

Well, Sancho had no appetite for fighting. Perhaps, he said, there was some sort of fine that he could pay. "In any case, I have no weapon with me."

"Well, we can fight with cotton bags – a bag fight," said the Forest Squire.

"This I'll do," said Sancho. "The only outcome will be dusty jackets."

"We'll fill the bags with pebbles," said the Forest Squire. "And that way we'll be injured just a little."

"I will not fight," said Sancho. "As it is, Father Time will steal our lives away too soon. We do not need to think up ways to help him. In any case, I do not wish to fight a man who's been so generous with wine and pie. I will not fight without a cause of anger."

"Well, I will make it easier. Right before our knights begin their combat, I'll come to you and smack you several times upon the head. I'm sure that this will do to make you angry."

"On second thought," said Sancho, "I have a plan myself. Before you have a chance to land a blow, I'll grab a club and knock you on the head so hard, that when you do come back to life, you'll do so in the world that lies beyond."

Dawn came.

The dew dropped down to coat the grass with jewels. The birds began to trill and call above. The sun came up and Don Quixote and his squire finally set eyes on their opponents.

The Forest Knight was splendid to behold. He wore a golden cloak upon his armor, covered every inch with tiny spangles. Atop his golden helmet waved a crop of plumes. His lance was long and tipped with glinting steel. He was no more the Forest Knight, at least to Don Quixote's dazzled senses. Knight of The Spangles. That's the name we'll call him from now on.

"Remove your visor, sir," said Don Quixote. "I must know if your face is as noble as your overall appearance."

"I will not," was the reply. "I'll not delay this conquest for my Lady Fair. You'll see my face before the morning's done."

But, oh! Poor Sancho Panza. *His* adversary's face was now revealed, and Sancho might have wished it had been hidden. Though I run the risk of seeming harsh, the Forest Squire had a face of such surpassing ugliness that words will not suffice to call it up.

This ugliness – so sumptuous – resided in the Forest Squire's nose. This nose was so enormous that even by the light of day, his body, for the most part, lay in shade. Bigger than an eggplant was this nose and cruel fate had covered it in warts. It was purple, like an eggplant: nature had lost course and run amok.

Seeing this, Sancho shook and quailed, like a tiny child beset by fits.

As to the joust: the knights met at mid-field upon their horses, and, having met, they turned their animals to ride to their positions for the charge. This was the protocol at any joust. But as the knights rode off to take their starting points, Sancho let his dread and fear defeat him. He ran to catch his master by the stirrup.

"Master," pleaded Sancho, "before you turn about to charge, I beg you, help me up into a tree. I need to climb up high to watch the fight."

Of course, Quixote knew this was a ploy. He knew his squire was frightened of his counterpart. Still, Quixote stopped his horse. He would oblige. On this one day he showed his squire mercy.

Meanwhile, though, the Spangled Knight reached the place to turn his horse to charge. He turned his horse and raised his lance and kicked his steed, not noticing that his enemy had been delayed in reaching his position. Once galloping at full speed down the meadow, he saw (too late), that Don Quixote had not moved.

The Spangled Knight pulled up his horse abruptly, just as Don Quixote turned to charge.

Rocinante charged. The Spangled Knight now spurred his horse anew. Confused, the animal refused to budge. So Don Quixote reached his foe and struck his shining enemy full force, hurling the poor Spangled Knight upon his back, upon the ground. Defeated.

The Spangled Knight lay still. Had he been killed? He lay there – splendid to behold, and conquered. Don Quixote climbed down from his horse. He lifted up his adversary's visor. And whose familiar face did it reveal?

"Sancho!" cried Quixote. "Come and see what has been done by magic. Enchanters! They have made this fallen knight exactly like the Bachelor Carrasco. I would almost swear that it was he!"

"Shove your sword into his mouth!" said Sancho. It seems that fear had made the squire ruthless. "Run him through, in case he is not dead." He crossed himself (a man of Christian feeling) and crossed himself again.

Don Quixote lifted up his sword to strike. He'd snuff out this imposter who'd taken the appearance of his friend.

"Stop!" Just as Don Quixote would draw blood, a voice cried out.

The squire of the Spangled Knight came running – the squire of the Spangled Knight, who now appeared without his fearsome nose.

"It is the Bachelor Carrasco whom you've conquered. It is your friend who's dressed up as a knight. Stop!" he cried again.

"Where is your nose?" asked Sancho. (First things first.)

"In my pocket" said the squire. From deep within his garments the squire brought a lumpy purple mask.

Sancho Panza recognized the squire. "You are my neighbor! You are Tome Cecial."

Quixote took this in and mulled it over. How could these strange events be understood? It was true the Forest Squire looked just like their good neighbor from La Mancha. And the fallen Spangled Knight – he did look like the Bachelor Carrasco. But Don Quixote did not trust his senses, and he made up his mind he'd not be tricked. This was not the Bachelor Carrasco at his feet. It was an enchanter in the dirt, whom Don Quixote now deigned to address.

"You must confess," Quixote said, "my Lady Fair is peerless in her beauty. She surpasses by a thousand fold the beauty of your Lady Fair. As for the task I'll set you, you will depart for El Toboso, where you will tell my Lady Dulcinea you've been conquered in her name. You will perform whatever thing she asks."

The fallen knight made not a single argument. He found his feet. Squinting in the morning sun he limped away, angry, vengeance surging in his heart, supported by his squire (who one day would be high up in the church and looked for all the world like Sancho's neighbor).

Don Quixote Becomes the
Knight of The Lions

൜

Quixote and his squire climb on their horse and ass and set about to take the road. As they can no longer hear us, the time arrives for readers to be told the truth. It was, indeed, the Bachelor Carrasco whom Don Quixote conquered in the woods. His squire was the neighbor named Cecial.

How was this? Before Quixote and his squire had left La Mancha, bound for their adventures, the Bachelor had come up with a scheme to bring them home. He told the priest and barber of his plan. (He hadn't taxed the ladies by informing them.) The Bachelor would dress up like a knight and follow Don Quixote and his squire. When the time was right, he'd challenge Don Quixote to a fight. Of course, he'd win. He didn't doubt that he'd defeat Quixote.

As victor, he'd demand that Don Quixote go back to La Mancha for two years.

There are circumstances in the world that everyone agrees require knights. Let's say a princess is abducted, a giant who is murderous appears, an orphan or a widow is endangered, a Lady's spotless virtue is impugned. These are challenges that call for knights. The rest of us stand back. We read along. We wish them well.

And then there is another sort of mission. A knight, with knightly knowledge we don't share, will spot an undertaking meant for knights alone. He'll see the signs that you and I might miss.

Finally, it turns out there's another sort of task that only Don Quixote could discern. Having more than his fair share of knightly knowledge, Quixote could see subtle hints that other knights would possibly have missed.

Let's take our next adventure as example. Another knight might have ignored the cart that now came into view along the road. To most eyes it would probably seem innocent – a cart adorned with royal flags, hurting no one, going on its way.

But when he saw the royal cart, Don Quixote stopped at full alert. "Here I stand," he said, "ready, if I must, to battle Satan!"

Satan?

The cart bore two large crates, and riding on the crates there were two carters.

"Whither are you going?" asked the knight. "What cart is this? Whose flags are these? Please tell me."

One of the carters told the knight that the crates held two grown lions – gifts they were conveying to the king. They had traveled all the way from North Africa. And would Quixote step aside and let them pass?

The knight would not, for Don Quixote knew full well that it is commonplace for knights to battle lions. He knew it, for he'd read it in his books. If there were lions in the crates, then they were meant to die beneath his sword.

"Uncrate the beasts!" Quixote boomed. "I will let them understand what it is to battle Don Quixote. I know it is enchanters who have sent them."

But the carter who addressed the knight was on a pressing mission of his own; to take the lions to the king. Then, as now, the carter knew it's never wise to disappoint a monarch. He would not let the lions out.

"Uncrate the beasts!" said Don Quixote to the carter. "Or I will take my lance and pin you to the crate." Don Quixote raised his lance to strike.

And so the carter, shuddering with fear, delivering a stream of frantic warnings, consented.

Sancho begged the knight to change his mind. "This is more dangerous than anything you've ever done. It is one thing to fight with windmills and with fulling mills and sheep, but you will die if you pick fights with lions."

Quixote paid his squire no attention. The carter, quailing at the coming danger, untied his mules and struck them in the rear to make them run. Sancho spurred on Dapple to put whatever distance possible between them – man and donkey – and the bloodbath which would be upon them. The second carter opened up the rearmost crate.

Quixote jumped down from his horse, threw aside his lance, lifted up his sword and shield, and advanced upon the opened door to meet his foe.

She was indeed a mighty beast, a great and brawny lion, a fitting gift to offer up to royalty. She shifted in her crate to face the knight. The creature, it turns out, had been asleep. She opened up her eyes and brought her gaze to rest upon Quixote.

The gaze – the coal black eyes – darkness of the jungle come to Spain. The lioness looked upon the knight, then looked about outside the crate, her eyes like scorching torches, back and forth. She stretched a paw. She opened up her giant jaws. Who would not tremble at this awesome sight? She brought forth her enormous tongue to wash her face. She shifted forward in the crate, raised up her head and looked about again. She yawned.

Don Quixote, steadfast, waited bravely at the open door. Quixote, the great and famous knight – fearless, with his blood aboil, his shield aloft, his sword held high, awaited battle with the giant beast. He would reduce his foe to bits and pieces. Oh, he would set this monster's blood aflow.

The lioness, however, looked on Don Quixote – this shriveled human beast with sword unsheathed – and didn't find him terrible at all. She stood up for the time it took to turn around, and calmly flung herself back down to rest. She groaned and sighed and shut her blazing eyes.

It seems she did not know, as Don Quixote did, that knights and lions, when they meet, must do their best to tear each other limb from limb. (Humankind: we know these things, because we are – of all the beasts – most clever.)

Here was her hind end, if he would fight it – magnificent, but offering no contest.

"You must beat her," called Quixote to the carter. "Beat her, so she will come out to fight me."

The carter was intelligent, however, and came up with the very thing to say.

"You have challenged her. No one could ever say you are a coward. You need not strike the lion. Think of this as though she were a foe who did not come at the appointed hour to fight a duel. The lioness has forfeited the fight. You are the victor, Don Quixote. You have offered her a battle. If she does not fight you, you have won."

With this inspired bit of logic on the carter's part, the showdown with the fearsome beast was done. The carter closed the crate. Sancho and the animals returned. Quixote was victorious and proud.

"I will take up another name," Quixote said. "I will henceforth be called Knight of The Lions. It will tell the world of my great conquest."

And while it's true the battle could have been more heated, it's also true (to give the knight his due), that Quixote could not possibly have been more brave. It was pure chance the beast was very sleepy. Many lions would have shown more interest.

The Cave of Montesinos

The next few days brought nothing but good fortune. Our heroes took the road again and came upon a wedding in the fields. We won't stop here to meet the bride and bridegroom. (Newlyweds get plenty of attention.) We'll only note their union resulted in a vast and splendid feast. Our heroes stayed three days, and when they left, their saddlebags were filled with every kind of thing to eat and drink.

But Don Quixote and his squire left with something much more precious than provisions. There was a scholar at the celebration, an expert on the Cave of Montesinos, a nearby cavern in the earth, reputed to be several miles deep.

If you haven't heard of it, please take my word, it was known to the people of that time and place. And Don Quixote – curious, intelligent, possessor of a questing, restless heart – felt its magic tug, and very keenly. He would brave its mysteries.

"You will be stuck down there," said Sancho, worrying as always, for his master, "like a bottle that's been lowered in a well to cool."

The scholar said that he would come along.

The knight, the squire, and the scholar made their way toward the cave, stopping in a village only long enough to buy a length of rope. It was within a day or so, they came upon the entrance of the cave.

The Cave of Montesinos. It was very famous – a legend – yet, from all appearances, nobody had been there for some time. Its mouth was woven closed with weeds and vines, with brambles and with wild figs and buckthorn.

Don Quixote would not be deterred. The knight brought out his rope. The scholar and the squire tied one end around him. Two hundred yards of rope they'd brought. They did not know if this would be enough.

"I pray you," the scholar said, "examine with one hundred eyes the things below."

Quixote did not answer. He sank down to his knees. He sent up to his Lady Fair these words that he believed might be his last: "Oh peerless Dulcinea. If my prayers might reach thine ears, refuse me not thy favor and protection. I am about to sink myself in the abyss, to make it known throughout the world that thou dost favor me. For you, there is no fear that is beyond me."

His supplications done, Don Quixote set about a battle with the brambles, to open up the cavern's gloomy jaws. By Don Quixote's sword the cave was breeched.

How much time had passed since any other person had cut these thorns for access? So long, that in these weeds and vines, a colony of crows and bats had made a home. At the strike of Don Quixote's sword they rose as one, rushing from a thousand places down below. Rising by the hundreds. Rushing upward from the dark, they jostled Don Quixote and threw our rope-bound hero to the ground. A cloud of black, they rose and called and tilted in the sky. To anyone with sense within their head, this rush of wings, this noise of disconcerted creatures would be warning.

Sancho and the scholar lowered Don Quixote on the rope. Sancho sent his prayers up with the ravens.

"May God above look after you!" cried Sancho. "Oh, flower of knights-errant, with heart of steel and arm of bronze."

Don Quixote dropped into the dark. He called as he descended, beckoning his friends to pay out rope. His voice grew fainter as he sank. It was as though he called up through a funnel. Fifty feet. One hundred feet. Down and down into the dark. On and on, until the rope was spent.

At the entrance to the cave, Sancho and the scholar held the rope. They peered into the blackness of the cavern.

No sound. They waited half an hour. They waited for as long as they could bear it. They tugged the rope. It bore no weight. Had Don Quixote somehow come unfastened?

Tears welled up in Sancho Panza's eyes. The men began to gather rope in earnest. Faster and then faster. Ten feet and then twenty feet and thirty. Then finally, they felt a weight take hold.

Straining, weeping, overjoyed, the scholar and the squire hauled upon the rope with all their might.

"Welcome back!" called Sancho down the hole. But there was no sound from Don Quixote. When finally he did appear it looked, for all the world, like he was sleeping.

They brought Quixote out and they untied him. They laid the knight upon the ground. He made no sound. His eyes were closed. He did not stir.

They rolled him back and forth.

Finally, thank Him above who looks down with such tenderness upon us, Don Quixote opened up his eyes.

"May God above forgive you." Bleary-eyed, he looked into their faces.

"God forgive the both of you for taking me from the most delightful life that any man has ever lived, from the most delicious sights I've ever seen. Now I understand," he said, "that all of the pleasures of this life must pass away, must wither like the flowers of the field, must disappear like shadows or a dream."

Well, this is true enough. (Some would say that this is even obvious.) But what had made Quixote know it now?

Dear Reader, Don Quixote will tell us what miracles he came upon within the cave. He'll tell us and he'll tell the squire and scholar. But we will have to wait a moment longer. Don Quixote, possessor of a questing heart, just this once insisted he was hungry. Just this once, he had a questing stomach.

The three took out their saddlebags and spread out their provisions on the grass. By four o'clock the meal was done and by the amber light of afternoon, Don Quixote wiped his mouth and undertook the story of the cave.

One moment though: The translator would like another word with us. He'd have us know that he does not believe the tale that Don Quixote is about to tell. The story is improbable. He includes it, he explains — he feels he must — but says he cannot vouch for it as truth.

And now the translator has had his say, we can proceed to hear Quixote's story, from the moment of his entrance to the cave.

Down, down went Don Quixote in the dark, spinning, dangling, turning on the rope. Down he went, trussed up. Down he went, leaving daylight up above, dropping all alone into the cave, dropping like a spider on a filament of web. Finally, he'd dropped so far he started to suspect there was no bottom to the cave at all. But just as this idea dawned upon him, suddenly he saw a shaft of light.

"There I found a recess on the cavern walls," Quixote said, "large enough to hold a cart and mules. I perched upon the ledge and called to you. I think you did not hear me. I coiled up the rope that dropped behind me, and then I fell into a state of rumination and, from that state, into a sort of trance."

"And when I woke," he told the squire and scholar, "I found I was no longer in the cave."

He opened up his eyes and looked around. He blinked his eyes and opened them up wider. It was some sort of paradise he woke to – a meadow, so delightful and so beautiful it was beyond what any mind could conjure up. A green and sunlit meadow, underground.

"I looked around," Quixote said, "and there across the meadow was a castle." A castle made of bright and sparkling crystal. A castle caught by sunlight down within the bowels of the earth! The castle's gates drew open. A dignified old man came out the doors. It seems that Don Quixote was expected.

Dignified old men who lived down in the bowels of the earth dressed splendidly, according to this story. This one had a trailing purple cloak, a satin stole around his spavined shoulders. On his head he wore a round, black cap. His gray beard trailed to well below his waist.

He made his way across the field and introduced himself as Montesinos.

"We've waited for you in this lonely place. For it's your task to hear our tale and take our story to the world above us. Please follow me into the crystal castle."

To anyone who's versed in Spanish ballads, the characters we'll meet here are familiar. Certainly Quixote knew their names from songs that had been sung for generations.

Known to each and every Spanish child was a fabled knight named Durandarte. When Durandarte was about to die, he'd made a memorable and grim request. He asked his friend and cousin, Montesinos, this: once he'd breathed his last, Montesinos was to take a knife and cut into his lifeless chest. His heart was to be taken out and given to his lover as a gift. This would show the lady that Durandarte loved her – that she would everlastingly posses his heart, no matter that his heart had ceased to beat.

Loyal Montesinos had done as he'd been asked. He'd taken out his cousin's bleeding heart, wrapped it up in linen, sprinkled it with salt to keep it fresh, and taken it to Durandarte's Lady Fair: a beauty beyond measure named Belerma. But the story had not ended there. A powerful magician known as Merlin had got it in his head to interfere.

Evil Merlin cast a spell, and so it was that Durandarte

did not fully die. His heart had been removed and taken to his Lady Fair as bidden, but the noble knight had been enchanted. He lay upon a marble tomb within the sparkling castle underground, not moving, but still made of warm and living flesh. And thus he had remained four hundred years. From time to time his body sighed and moaned.

Durandarte did not turn to dust as we are meant to do. And Montesinos and Belerma did not die at all. Nor did their sorry retinue of servants. Instead they all grew very very old.

In the crystal castle, Montesinos and Quixote made their way to Durandarte's tomb. There he lay, as though he were asleep. But he was not at rest. He was a breathing corpse beset by nightmares. Durandarte, on his marble tomb, whispered bits of verse, asking that his heart be taken out and given to his Lady Fair Belerma.

As Don Quixote and the old man watched, Belerma came into a hall nearby. There she was beyond a crystal wall. She followed two long lines of servant maidens, dressed in deepest mourning, as was she.

In her hands Belerma held her lover's heart. Faithful, she had loved him these four hundred years.

But time had not stood still for poor Belerma. The years had etched her face and leached her vigor; had tugged her flesh and bent her back. Her skin was pale and sickly, her eyes were smudged with shadows underneath. Her eyebrows had grown long and joined together, bulging overtop a swollen nose. Her teeth, though white, had shifted, leaving gaps. Her mouth was big and slack and much too red. Long ago, she'd reached the age when she could not have children. She was a sight her lover would not have known.

Up above the cavern on the grass the squire and the scholar had listened to the knight's unlikely tale. The amber afternoon began to cool. Finally, the scholar had a question.

"How can it be," the scholar asked, "that all of this took place so very quickly?"

"So quickly?" Don Quixote asked. "Night came and went three times while I was underground."

Puzzlement and silence. Then the scholar had another question: "Did you eat in all that time?" A scholar, he was curious for details.

"Not in three days," Quixote said.

"Do the enchanted eat at all?" the scholar asked.

"No," Quixote told him. "Nor do they feel the callings of the bladder and the bowel, although it's said their hair and their fingernails and toenails still grow."

Now it was Sancho's turn to interject. "I'm sure you will forgive me if I point out this story is ridiculous. Perhaps you did not eat in three long days, but enchanters surely stuffed your head with nonsense."

"Not so," said Don Quixote. "I'm telling you exactly what I saw. And there is more. For whom else did I meet there but my Lady Fair, my peerless Dulcinea, and the peasant girls we met with her before. All were just exactly as we saw them last, capering like she-goats in the field. I called to Dulcinea, but she ran from me so fast, a speeding arrow never could have caught her. And soon one of her servant girls came circling back. She said her lady wished to borrow money. I gave the servant everything I had, and sent along a message that, on my honor as a knight, I would see her mistress disenchanted."

"Well, now I know that you have lost your wits," said Sancho. "For God's sake, keep this story to yourself."

"I know," said Don Quixote to his squire, "you say these things because you truly love me, and because you know so little of the world. Things that you don't understand you set aside and say they are impossible. Whatever you will make of this: there is good news. Montesinos told me I will find a way to rescue Dulcinea from her spell."

The translator now interrupts again to tell us Don Quixote, on his deathbed, admitted that this story was invented.

Did Don Quixote lie? Was he mistaken? Was it on his deathbed that he lied? Or on that afternoon outside the cave? And why would he have made up such a tale? How can we know? The truth is that we never will. In life we must content ourselves with guessing.

The Story of the Village
of the Bray; A Puppet Show.

The world is so miraculous and strange. Even when enchantment's not afoot, there is so much to dazzle and bewilder us. But day-to-day realities will always stake their claim upon our thoughts.

And so it was this day. Our heroes – Don Quixote, Sancho Panza, and, just for now, the scholar, needed somewhere they could spend the night.

They packed their things and left the cave and carried on. But fresh events were soon to overtake them. Along the road behind them, came a stranger. He was in a hurry and walked behind a mule who was laden with a vast supply of weapons, bristling like a porcupine with lances and with halberds. A halberd is a lance that bears an axe.

The man whose beast this was, was beating the poor creature with a stick.

"Stop!" said Don Quixote. "Where are you going?

Why such haste? You seem to travel faster than your mule would wish."

"These weapons," said the stranger, "are needed for a battle. I must reach the inn ahead by nightfall. If you wish, I'll tell you of my business then." He hurried off along the road.

That night, when Don Quixote's party reached the inn, they found the fellow working in the stable, seeing to the comfort of his mule. (The mule whom he'd been beating with a stick!) Don Quixote, Sancho Panza, the innkeeper, and scholar listened as the stranger told his tale.

Fifteen miles away there lay a village where recently, by virtue of the hijinks of a servant girl, a donkey went astray. The beast had been the chattel of a councillor – a lofty local figure of some kind.

For two long weeks the animal was missing. For two weeks there was no word of his fate. And then one day, it seems another councillor (this village had important men to spare) saw the donkey in a local wood. It was the missing donkey without question. He still had on his saddle and his halter. But the animal escaped a second time. He ran off to take cover in the trees. Together the two councillors devised a plan to catch the wayward beast.

One councillor would take a path around the wood; his friend would walk the path the other way. Both of them would bray just like a donkey. If the missing beast was in the wood the fugitive would bray, thinking he was answering a donkey. Thus the councillors would find out where the animal was hiding.

At the outskirts of the wood, the two set out in opposite directions. The councillors brayed loudly, and both were soon rewarded with an answer. Success! They hurried to the place from whence the call had come, and there among the trees they found . . . each other.

Now, their plan had failed to yield the donkey, but neither of them was the least downhearted. In fact, they'd found a cause for celebration. How well they'd done, the men agreed, in mimicking the outbursts of a donkey!

"Can it be you who brayed?" asked one. "As far as braying goes, I've never heard anything so convincing."

"By God who made me," said his friend. "I think that you were twice as good as I. Perfect pitch and just the proper tempo. And the very rhythm of a donkey. The way that you sustained the phrase. The cadenza. The ornamentation you devised! Bravo!"

"I will admit," the first confessed, "I must agree. I knew that I could bray, but didn't know that I had this much talent."

Their mutual congratulations over, the two resumed the search. They tried their plan a second time, but met up with each other as before. Once more they tried, and found themselves again come face-to-face. And then the gifted fellows took another tack. This time (their fourth!), they would call out in double-brays, letting out two blasts in quick succession. By doing so, they'd recognize the other's call. They'd not mistake the other for an ass. And so, on this their last attempt, the two did not repeat the same mistake. But there was still no answer from the missing beast. As a last-ditch measure they walked into the wood and looked around. There he was, the missing ass – dead and rotten, half consumed by wolves.

To you and me this is no happy ending, but returning to the village, the councillors who told their tale, carried on as if they'd won the day. The donkey was no more, it's true, but the two could cheerfully report that they had come upon their hidden talents. Both could bray exactly like a donkey! In itself it was a sort of triumph.

⁀ᴍᴍꞔ

"The devil never sleeps" they used to say. Before too long the story spread. People from the nearby towns made merry of the councillors' success. Before too long, whenever someone from the missing donkey's village ventured out, the people of these other towns would bray. The donkey's town was now renamed. People called it Village of the Bray.

Teasing led to anger (as it tends to do), anger led to skirmishes, and then to full blown fights. In fact (so said the stranger to our heroes), there would be a battle in a day or so. The lances and the halberds that the stranger brought were weapons for the Village of the Bray.

So the story ended in the innyard. But new events awaited in the wings.

"Landlord! Tell me," called a voice from somewhere on the outskirts of the yard. "Do you have rooms tonight? The puppet show and fortune-telling ape are on their way."

The puppet show! The fortune-telling ape! The innkeeper was utterly delighted at this news.

The voice we've heard from just offstage belonged to someone known as Master Pedro. And Master Pedro was a well-known fellow. Master Pedro was a puppeteer. For a fee, abetted by his servant, this artist would put on a puppet play. But even more exciting than the puppets was Master Pedro's fortune-telling ape.

Master Pedro came into the yard, his face half-hidden by a veil of silk. "Master Pedro," said the innkeeper. "What pleasures are in store for us tonight? To take you in, I'd toss the finest duke out on his ear."

The company came into the yard. And here he was, the magic ape, riding with the puppets in a cart, pushed by Master Pedro and his helper.

The ape was large and had no tail. His buttocks, we are told, were like old leather. But shall we shift our focus to his other end? His face. It was a sight that caught one quite off-guard. His face – the ape's – was curious and kindly and knowing and intelligent and wise.

Of course, the group was eager for his wisdom. So seldom does an ape reveal his thoughts. Don Quixote was the first in line.

"What will become of all of us?" he asked the ape.

"No," said Master Pedro, before the ape could summon a response. "The ape cannot tell things about the future. His specialty is past events and present day."

"What good is that?" asked Sancho. "I wouldn't give a farthing to be told what's happened in the past. I know the past already. But here's a little pocket change. Ask the monkey what my wife is doing."

"No," said Master Pedro. "Keep your money for the moment. I'll take it if the ape provides an answer."

At this the puppet master lifted up his hand and tapped himself two times upon the shoulder. The ape, who had been paying close attention, jumped up and put his mouth beside his master's head. He chattered with his teeth into his master's ear.

Master Pedro listened to the chattering, and as he did, his eyes grew wide and wider. His gaze left Sancho Panza's face and fixed with rapt delight on Don Quixote. Master Pedro dropped down to his knees and wrapped his arms about Quixote's legs.

"I embrace these noble legs as though they were the twin pillars of Hercules. Reviver of the Order of Knight-Errantry! Magnificent Quixote, friend to the fainthearted, support of those about to fall, helper of the downtrodden, comfort to the needy and the weak.

"And you," said Master Pedro, now turning to the squire, "the greatest squire who ever served a knight. The ape reports your wife is well. Just now she's carding flax outside your cottage door and keeping up her spirits with a jug of wine."

Don Quixote and the squire, the arms bearer, the innkeeper, and scholar were astonished. Was it true the wise and kindly ape had recognized our heroes by himself? It really seemed quite possible he had.

"Tonight for Don Quixote," said the puppeteer, "I will perform the show for free."

Now, for all that Master Pedro was clearly overjoyed to meet Quixote (for all that this was flattering and fitting), the episode had made the knight uneasy. *Somehow*, thought Quixote, *these doings are too magical for comfort.* While Master Pedro and his servant set their stage and readied all the puppets for the play, Don Quixote had a word with Sancho.

"It's possible," Quixote said, "this man has made a compact with the devil, to have an ape with talents such as these. Gifts so great are seldom come by honestly. I fear that Master Pedro might have traded in his soul for the fortune that a magic ape would bring."

"This could be true," said Sancho, "but all the same, I'd like to ask the ape more questions. I'd like to know, for one thing, if what you tell us happened in the Cave of Montesinos was the truth. With all respect, I still believe your story must be some sort of trick, or lie, or dream."

And so it was that before the show, the ape was called upon again by Master Pedro, and asked about the Cave of Montesinos. The ape jumped up and chattered in his master's ear.

"The ape," said Master Pedro, "says that part of what Don Quixote tells us of the Cave is true and part is not. The ape knows this and nothing else. And now, my friends, his powers are exhausted. He won't have further insights until Friday."

Some of it was true and some was not.

But let's return to real events: the puppet show. The time has come to take our seats.

⌒⌒⌒

The puppet stage was glorious, shining with a multitude of candles. Master Pedro hid himself to animate the puppets from behind. Out in front, his servant boy prepared to tell the puppets' story. He held a wand with which to point out features in the plot he would have the audience pay heed to.

Guns rang out, and trumpets. There were war drums and the tale began.

A woman, Melisedra, was kidnapped by a brutish band of Moors. Poor soul. Poor lovely thing in dire need of rescue! But her husband, Don Gaiferos, did not undertake to chase her captors – not at first. He was busy, much too busy. He was busy playing board games with his friends. So we find him when the play begins.

The servant boy indicates the lazy puppet husband with his wand.

Now, the stolen lady's father was an emperor. There he is. The servant boy moves his wand to point him out. This emperor, the great and mighty Charlemagne, demands in an angry tone of voice that his son-in-law must venture forth, even if it means that Don Gaiferos' board games would be put aside. We look on as the puppet Charlemagne beats young Don Gaiferos with his scepter. Soon the lazy husband leaves his games behind.

The puppet husband is astride his horse. The servant sweeps his wand across the stage to show us where the damsel waits for rescue.

She's trapped upon a balcony, on the farthest reaches of the stage. She's pestered by the amorous attentions of a guard. He presses an unwanted kiss upon her paper lips. He grasps her roughly (cardboard fiend), clasps her in his tiny, rustling arms.

Don Gaiferos finally arrives (puppet on a tiny puppet horse). Melisedra sees him and jumps from her balcony to meet him. For one heart-stopping moment her flowing dress is caught upon an iron rail. Don Gaiferos tears her from its grasp. She drops into the saddle right behind him. Off they go, a handsome sight, this puppet pair, galloping and galloping across the stage.

But listen! In the distance! Tiny Moorish bells ring out from tiny mosques. The little cardboard couple has been spotted. The Moors have sent an army to arrest them.

But then, out in the audience, Don Quixote shifted in his seat. "In mosques, there would be kettle drums instead," said Don Quixote. "In mosques they do not ring those tiny bells." He made this small complaint and then fell silent.

On the stage the story carries on.

Behold! We see the Moorish puppet army, rushing to recapture Melisedra.

The wand sweeps past to show us Don Gaiferos, riding like the wind across the stage. Behind him on his horse there is his frightened bride. Her dress is torn! The cavalry advances in the candlelight. Bells and gunshots, war drums, music, trumpets!

But what is this? At this most crucial moment of the drama, the action shifted out into the audience. Don Quixote's crankiness had blossomed into something like hysterics.

Wild with avenging knightly frenzy, Don Quixote rose. He drew his sword and rushed into the hoard of puppet Moors. Before his shocked companions could prevent it, he slashed and crushed the tiny troops, stopping their nefarious pursuit. He chopped off tiny heads from tiny necks. Tiny arms and legs flew through the air. The enemy was conquered by Quixote.

But Don Quixote's fury was not spent. In the heat and passion of the moment, he turned his sword to every puppet thing. Charlemagne went down beneath his sword. So succumbed the lazy puppet husband and even his so newly rescued bride.

Only when the puppets were in pieces, the stage laid waste – no more than shards and scraps – the audience uproarious, the ape gone out the window in a panic, and Master Pedro sobbing with his face held in his hands, did Don Quixote finally desist his puppet massacre to catch his breath.

"I hope," he said, "this will convince those who do not believe knights-errant are still necessary in this world."

Master Pedro wept. His puppets were destroyed. The

magic fortune-telling ape had disappeared. How was it that Quixote – so famous for his aid to the unfortunate – should have wrought such havoc for no cause?

Don Quixote stood amid the puppet dead and looked about, and as he did, his reeling world slowed down. What dreadful thing had taken place, he asked himself? His sword was raised. His heart was booming in his skinny chest. The reeling stopped. And then Quixote saw things as they were. Enchanters had bewitched him once again. Enchanters had convinced him that the play was real.

Bewildered and ashamed, Don Quixote scrambled for a way to make amends. He said that he would pay for all the puppets. Master Pedro, Sancho, and Quixote looked among the tiny cardboard corpses, discussing each small casualty one by one. They came up with a value for each victim and Don Quixote opened up his purse.

By morning the next day, the ape was back. The arms transporter packed his mule and left. The scholar from the wedding party bade goodbye to Don Quixote and his squire, and left for home. The puppet master and his servant and the ape gathered up the remnants of their show. Don Quixote (rightly so!) made a handsome payment to the innkeeeper. Our heroes once again were on their way.

As our heroes disappear from view, Mr. Benengeli interjects to tell us who the puppet master really was, and the truth about the fortune-telling ape.

Don Quixote and his squire once released a gang of hardened criminals because Quixote had decided they were blameless. They did this, you'll remember, in Book I. The worst of all these men — a criminal so dangerous his keepers had to lock him up with extra chains — had become the puppeteer, this character who's now called Master Pedro.

Master Pedro, Benengeli tells us, had lost his chains, but not his wicked nature. Before he entered any town, the puppeteer would make a few inquiries. He'd have a look around (his face half hidden by his silken mask) and find things out. Soon he'd know enough about the people in the town that he could trick them with his magic ape. The ape could not tell fortunes, but knew that when his master tapped his shoulder, the ape must appear to whisper in his master's ear.

The ape had seemed to recognize Quixote. But it was Master Pedro who had known him.

The riddle of the ape is hereby solved.

⟊⟊⟊

Dear Reader, are there fortune-telling apes out in the world? Perhaps there are, for all we know. But rest assured that Master Pedro's ape was never among them.

THE RIVER EBRO

Do you recall that Don Quixote had a plan to go to Saragossa for the jousting? He planned, as well (we learn this now), to pay a visit to the River Ebro. There were some days to spare before the contests. So to the river he and Sancho bent their course.

The journey to the River Ebro took two days, and when our heroes came upon the river's shores they were assailed, not by puppet villains, not by knights dressed up in sparkling armor, not by weeping housekeepers, not by angry bats and shrieking ravens, nor by misleading apes, but by sheer beauty.

The cool green banks, the glistening glinting waters, the river's sleepy flow. It was a pretty day, with breezes that push back your hair like fingers. Here was the beauty of the world, existing – whether seen by human eyes or not – with no apparent reason, no intention. And all at once, this loveliness – its mystery, the fact of its unlikely and astonishing existence – called Quixote's mind to mystic musings. His thoughts set out to wander, and found their way to landscapes of the past. Montesino's Cave, for one example. Had it been real? The ape had said the story had been partly true and partly not. Don Quixote tended to believe it had been real.

Musing thus, he saw a little boat upon the riverbank.

It had no oars. Don Quixote looked around for fishermen. It seemed the vessel had no owners, either. It was abandoned, tied up to a tree. Oh, plain as lovely day, Don Quixote knew the boat was meant for him to board.

"This boat is indication," said Don Quixote to his squire. "There is some knight, or other person of high rank, who needs our help." (Sancho needed everything spelled out.) "The books are full of stories of this kind. A knight who is required for such missions might be flown to his adventure through the clouds, or offered, as I am today, a boat. The boat will carry us away, perhaps a thousand miles, in no more than the twinkling of an eye. Magically, we'll speed to where we're needed. Tie up the beasts, and we will go aboard."

Now, Sancho knew that sometimes boats were only boats. "Forgive me," Sancho Panza said. "This boat seems much better suited to fishing than to flying through the air.

In fact, this is a famous place for catching shad. The fishermen are probably close by."

But Sancho might as well have saved his breath. Quixote was intent upon his mission.

With heavy heart, Sancho tied the horse and donkey to a tree. He dreaded being parted from the animals. Who would feed and water them? He knew that they would be confused and lonely. But Quixote would not listen to his squire.

"Whoever has contrived our task will care for them," Quixote said.

So, Don Quixote and the squire climbed aboard the boat. Dapple let out great heartbreaking moans. Rocinante fought against his ropes. Were they to be abandoned on the riverbank? Would this be their recompense for all their many years of loyal service?

As our heroes pushed away from shore, Sancho broke into a flood of tears.

"You coward" said Quixote. He didn't understand his squire's grief. "You butter-hearted baby, blubbering like this. Unless I am mistaken, no one's chasing you. You're drifting on a river, sitting on a bench like an archduke. And soon we'll both be sailing on a boundless sea!"

Don Quixote looked about; up and down the river, at the sky, taking measures, reckoning the wind and waves.

"In fact, we might have reached the sea already," said the knight. "I think we've traveled several thousand miles. By my calculations we might have almost come to the equator. And I can tell you (as you are a moron) how I know we've come this far. It's said that when you reach the earth's equator all the lice that live upon your person will expire. Sancho! Pass your hand across your thigh. See if any ticks remain within your clothes."

Sancho looked about him. The riverbank was still close by. Only five short feet away, the horse and donkey fought against their ropes and sent up cries.

"The boat has barely moved at all," said Sancho.

"You are ignorant," said Don Quixote. "Often you are misled by appearances. You do not know the ins and outs of solstices and equinoxes; of planets, signs and poles. You are ignorant of zodiacs and parallels and all the points and measurements of which the globe is made. You know nothing of the art of navigation. I tell you, once again, check yourself for lice! You will find them dead."

Sancho Panza did as he was told, but found his britches very much inhabited, a hive of great activity, every bit as populated as they ever were. They teemed with life, his trousers. Sancho plunged his hand into the river, setting tiny citizens adrift, exiles from the kingdom of his britches.

And then, despite the snail's pace of the voyage, the little boat went round the river bend. The setting for a new adventure drifted into place above the prow.

⟨≈⟩

Up ahead were water mills. But water mills, of course, need not be water mills. Not to the ingenious Quixote. They looked to Don Quixote like a city or a fortress or a castle. It also seemed quite obvious, by now, that in this place there was a knight or some exalted personage who needed help. Perhaps it was the infant daughter of a king. So explained Quixote to his squire. Poor child. A stolen baby! They must act!

"But this is not a fortress," said the squire. "Up ahead are water mills for grinding corn."

"They're water mills," explained the knight, "if you believe the fiction of enchanters."

Now, something one should keep in mind when drifting down a river to a water mill, is that these mills can grind up more than corn. They'll make short work of boats and sailors, too. The water mills churned round and round. In their little boat, Quixote and his squire grew ever closer. The boat began to hurry. The sleepy river woke and rushed along. And then from on the shore came shouts of warning.

Frantic workmen poured forth from the building, their faces white with flour, their voices raised, waving poles they'd brought to stop the boat.

"Monsters!" cried Quixote, for he mistook his rescuers for demons. "Blackguards, knaves, coming out to fight us! Sancho Panza! See their ugly faces – ashen, ghostly – if you doubt this is our proper mission."

"Ruffians!" he bellowed at the millers. "Release whatever prisoner you hold. For I am Don Quixote of La Mancha."

Don Quixote raised his sword.

Oh, it was very fortunate for him the millers could not hear a word he'd uttered. They only heard the tumult of the water. And luckily indeed, for Don Quixote, the millers, with the poles they'd brought, found a way to stop the boat in time.

But they could not prevent the boat's capsizing. Such was the power of the foaming water. Its passengers were thrown into the breech. Sancho Panza splashed and choked, fighting in the waves to stay afloat. And though Quixote could – as people of that time and place would put it – swim as deftly as a very goose, it's never wise to take a dip in armor. Twice, Quixote sank beneath the water. Twice, he struggled up in search of air.

Finally the demon millers pulled the knight and squire to shore. The fishing boat was shattered into splinters.

The shore. Dry land. The squire and the raving knight were saved. They lay upon the solid ground sodden to the skin (and not the least bit thirsty, says the book). Although he was fatigued beyond exhaustion, Sancho Panza found the strength to press his palms together in a prayer. Would God above, in future, save him from the knight's deluded schemes? For this he prayed with all his heaving heart.

I think we know his prayer will not be answered.

Suddenly more characters arrive: the fishermen, whose boat this was – whose boat was now in pieces in the foam. Who will pay? Whoever stole this boat must make amends.

"I'll pay," said Quixote to the group at large, addressing them from flat upon his back, "when you release whomever you've imprisoned."

Well, no one was imprisoned here. So explained the millers and the fishermen. Don Quixote pressed his case no further. "This adventure," said the knight, confessing to the sky above, "must have been intended for some other knight." Enchanters had misled him once again.

Don Quixote paid the fishermen. Then he and Sancho – sloshing, clanking, soaked – retreated up the river to their animals, who luckily were not too far away.

Through the forest, dark and wet, they made their way. Darling, dampened characters. Foggy thoughts among the misty trees.

We Meet the Duke
and Duchess

On the evening of the day that followed, the knight and squire reached the forest's edge. As dusk dropped down, they came upon a meadow. And there, across the meadow, dappled with the dimming light: a pretty scene, gentlefolk at play. There was a little crowd, and in its midst, a lady with a hawk. By virtue of her bearing, she seemed to be the leader of the party.

Don Quixote, in the proper way of knights, sent his squire up ahead to greet her.

"Tell her that I, Knight of The Lions, wish to kiss her hands. I salute her wondrous beauteousness and ask if I might serve her in some way."

Sancho rode across the field, and when he reached the lady with the hawk, he knelt before her. "My name is Sancho Panza. My master is the knight called Don Quixote, Knight of The Lions, who once was called Knight of Mournful

Countenance. He wishes he might serve your High and Mightiness."

Oh, well the lady knew the name! Quixote! She loved to read, this lady did, and she was up-to-date on every latest fashion on the shelves.

"Dear squire!" said the lady. "Can it be your master is the subject of that book *The Ingenious Gentleman Don Quixote of La Mancha*, whose lady is the famous Dulcinea del Toboso? Rise, dear squire. Please tell you master nothing could give me greater pleasure than to welcome him."

As Sancho Panza hurried back to take the lady's message to Quixote, the lady sent a message to her husband. He must come out to join her! That famous comic figure Don Quixote had fetched up in their own neck of the woods.

Her husband came as quickly as he could. He was a duke, her husband. The lady with the hawk, she was a duchess.

Don Quixote rode across the meadow with his squire. He stopped before the duchess, as solemn and as sober as a bishop – straight up in his saddle as a knight should be. But Sancho was his standard slapstick self.

Trying to dismount his ass, Sancho caught his foot and tumbled, winding up with one boot in its stirrups, face-down on the ground. Quixote, not noticing, thinking that his squire was in his proper place to hold Quixote's stirrups as he always did, swung himself with manly vigor from his horse. No luck today; his saddle had come loose. Quixote lost his footing. He ended up alongside Sancho Panza in the dirt.

How tickled was the little crowd of gentlefolk. There was no doubt this knight was Don Quixote – the character they'd so enjoyed in print. A world of fun lay crumpled at their feet! Falconry, this day, was put aside.

The ducal pair was lavish in their welcome. The duke made off to let the servants know they had a visitor, whom they must treat as if he were a knight from books. The Duchess, Sancho Panza, and Quixote followed, chatting on their horses as they rode.

Most amusing to the Duchess were Sancho Panza's loutish, comic ways. How delightful were his gaffes and tries at humor. He was every bit as quaint and entertaining – every bit the innocent she'd met between the pages of the book.

Emboldened by her obvious approval, Sancho prattled on; held center stage. This night, he knew, they'd have a proper dinner.

⚭

If ever Don Quixote had a doubt – and in his secret heart I think he had – that he was the knight he claimed to be, the question would be put aside this day. His reception at the palace was everything a famous knight could hope for. The servants came to greet him. Two lovely maidens met him in the courtyard and draped his meager frame with splendid robes. Maidservants and manservants sprinkled him with aromatic waters. They welcomed him and took him up the stairs.

Sancho Panza's entrance to the palace, on the other hand, did not go as smoothly as his master's. Arriving in the courtyard, feeling very grand – companion of a duchess as he was – he took it as his right to issue orders. His donkey needed tending to. And right away. He said this to the duchess' duenna. Sancho, coming in the gates had spotted her at once and caught her eye.

⁓

Just a moment to explain duennas. A duenna was a lady, often somewhat on in years, who was the friend and confidante and helper to the lady of the house. She only served the mistress of the household. She did not need to kowtow to the men. Because of this, the gentlemen would sometimes find her irksome. Or, let's say, they didn't see the point of creatures such as she – usually not young, no longer pretty, and sometimes rather nettlesome as well.

"Please have my donkey taken to the stables," said the squire. "Have it done, or take him there yourself. My donkey becomes frightened very easily. I will not have him left out all alone."

The duenna took exception, as you might predict, to loud and filthy squires with commands.

"A plague on you," she answered. "Duennas in this household don't tend donkeys."

The duchess intervened and stopped the quarrel, but word of it soon spread about the house.

And so when Don Quixote and the squire were reunited in their room, Don Quixote took the squire to task.

"Will you tell me, dunderhead and nincompoop and jester, did you think it proper form to insult the duchess' duenna? Can you not control yourself? Let's not have these people discover what a lowborn boob and bumbling half-wit peasant you are! They'll see me as a charlatan or as some third-rate, humbug knight. Try, for once, to stop your wagging tongue."

And with these words, the two went down to dinner.

Two rows of maidens met them in the hall. They carried bowls of water for the guests to wash their hands. Twelve pages had the privilege of escorting our two heroes to the table. There was pomp and ceremony as they advanced along the hall, curtsying and courtesies and such.

Within the ducal dining room places had been set for the duke and duchess, for Don Quixote, and for Sancho Panza. Also in attendance was a character who was a commonplace on great estates. He was a clergyman – a sour sort of gentleman, essential to the dampening of spirits of households that wished to be genteel.

More courtesies, more compliments. And then the duke, a gracious host, offered his own seat to Don Quixote.

Now, Don Quixote simply could not take it. He felt that it was not his place to do so. A contest of propriety ensued. Eventually it was the duke who got his way, insisting that the knight, as guest, must head the table, until Quixote had no other choice.

All of which reminded Sancho Panza of a charming story he'd once heard.

"It happened in my village," Sancho said, "and has to do with who sits where – a situation very much like this. An *hidalgo*, and a fine man to be sure, asked a local farmer to his table. Who would take the most important seat? Both men were very courteous. The *hidalgo* said, 'It is my house. I do insist you take the table head.' The farmer, who took pride in his respect for proper protocol, did not want to act above his station. He said that he could not accept the honor. Back and forth the matter went as dinner cooled upon the plates. Finally, the host ran out of patience. He placed his hands upon the farmer's shoulders and roughly shoved him down onto his seat. 'Sit down, you nincompoop,' he said. 'It doesn't matter where you sit. Where I sit is always table's head.'"

Don Quixote turned a thousand colors. The duke and duchess did their best to keep their faces straight. How thoroughly diverting was this Sancho. The silly squire was all that they had hoped.

With Sancho Panza's storytelling over, the conversation turned to Dulcinea. Don Quixote told his hosts the story of his many deeds on her behalf, how he had conquered giants for her glory and then, of the enchantment that had robbed her of her beauty, and of their meeting outside El Toboso.

Giants and enchantment? Dulcinea? The clergyman, who had been very quiet, began to listen closely to their talk. For it began to dawn on him exactly who these dinner guests might be. He knew them now. These were the heroes from a well-known book. And unless he was mistaken, it was a book that had no aim to edify the souls of those who read it. It was a book he'd begged the duke to set aside. It was a book of chivalry. Such books were often bawdy and immoral. (Or so he'd heard. By no means would he read one.)

He turned to Don Quixote.

"These books are lies and nonsense," said the man of God. "Go home," he said. "Who put it in your head you are a knight? Go home and tend your property and livestock. Can you believe these tales you tell are true?"

But Don Quixote would not be rebuked. Angrily the knight spoke to defend himself. "Who are you to judge the deeds of knights? You, who know so little of the world? I have brought down giants, righted wrongs and trampled monsters, and always chosen tribulation over ease. Your mission, on the other hand, is to join in on the dinnertimes of other men and rule on matters you don't understand."

"Well said!" Sancho Panza rallied to the knight's defense. "There's no doubt this fellow does not know of what he speaks."

"And who are you?" the clergyman demanded. "The Sancho Panza of the book who thinks that he will someday rule an island?"

"I am," said Sancho Panza.

"And so he will," the duke joined in. "I possess some islands. There is one to spare – and not a bad one. Sancho, here, will have it for his own."

At this, the man of God could take no more. He rose and spat out insults at the diners – some directed to his hosts; some of them were for their newfound friends. He gathered all his seemliness around him and stormed out of the house. He could not break his evening bread with such rebellious, unrepentant souls. The duke had disappointed him. The clergyman was usually obeyed.

Once the man of God had left the house, the talk returned to knightly things and, once again, to Lady Dulcinea.

"When she is not enchanted," said Quixote, "she is so fair that I cannot describe her. I wish I could pluck out my heart and lay it on the table here before you. My heart would tell the tale of how I love her. Only our great orators could come close to calling up what she was before magicians marred her – before she was enchanted and turned into a peasant from a princess."

"One moment," said the duke, remembering the details of Quixote's book. "It is possible my memory deceives me. Does it not say in your famous book that you have never actually laid eyes on her? May I ask you, Don Quixote, is it possible that she does not exist?"

"Well," said Don Quixote, "there's much that can be said on that account. These are certainly the sorts of things that someday should be investigated fully. But whether she exists or not, it truly can be said that she possesses every quality to make her justly famous through the world: beauty without flaw, dignity without pride. She is virtuous and gracious and courteous and noble and intelligent. And I shall live in floods of tears until the day I see her disenchanted."

"God bless you," said the duchess. "From this time on, I and all the members of my household shall believe that

Dulcinea del Toboso does exist, and must be all that you describe and more."

With dinner done, Don Quixote left the group and climbed the stairs to rest.

Left alone at last with Sancho Panza, the duke and duchess wanted all the details of the lovely Lady Dulcinea. Sancho rose and put his finger to his lips to quiet them. He made his way around the room on tiptoe, looking with great care behind each chair. He checked behind each tapestry upon the walls. Once satisfied that there was no one listening, he sat down.

Sancho Panza told his hosts how he had tricked Quixote in the field, that he had picked a peasant girl and told his master she was Dulcinea.

The duchess listened carefully. Her face showed only friendship for the squire, but back behind her shining eyes and friendly face, her shifty, crafty brain was hard at work. She had it on authority, she said, from an enchanter whom she knew would tell the truth, the peasant girl indeed *was* Dulcinea.

"You think that you've misled the knight," the duchess said. "The truth is, though, that by mistake you told the truth."

He'd told the truth by accident!

"Then perhaps," said Sancho, whose faith in his perceptions was shaken by this unexpected news, "it's possible as well, that the story Don Quixote tells of the Cave of Montesinos did take place."

The Cave of Montesinos?

"Please tell me," said the duchess. "What's this about the Cave of Montesinos?"

Warming to his newfound role – the intimate and confidante of duchesses – Sancho told the couple everything the knight had said he'd seen within the cave.

The Hunt; Merlin Appears
in the Wood.

∾

The duke had made it very clear to the servants: Quixote would be given every courtesy owing to a legendary knight. The duke and duchess pulled out all the stops. Good food and drink and comforts and amusements. Among the latter, one day, was a hunt.

The duke and duchess provided Don Quixote with a handsome hunting coat, but Quixote could not bring himself to take it. Knights should not be burdened down with gifts. But Sancho Panza had no qualms. He took his brand-new coat of worsted wool and put it on. He'd wear it for the moment. Someday he'd find a proper time to sell it.

The duke and duchess rode out to the field. As always, they were glamorous and gay. Alongside, rode a group of servant hunters and with them rode the beaters, whose job it was to crash about within the bush to frighten all the animals into the open for the hunters. There was clamor on all sides, the shouting and the calling of the hunters, the barking of the dogs, and the blasting and the bleating of the horns.

Soon enough a boar emerged; a large and hairy pig. He ran, poor beast, to meet the hunters' swords – ran full tilt, his eyes rolled back, his pounding pointy feet a thrumming blur. Here he came, chased by dogs and men, spittle spraying from his mouth, and mad with fear.

The boar was killed and slung upon a mule, and hunters covered up the beast with rosemary and myrtle. They took him to the clearing where the people of the duke's estate would dine.

It was a triumph for the little party. (Hunters like to make believe the fight is fair.) But Sancho did not share the cheerful mood. Frightened by the charging pig, he'd climbed into a tree and torn his coat.

"Lords and kings should not," he said, "put themselves at risk like this simply for the fun of killing animals who have not committed any crimes."

Sancho, friend to animals? While Sancho had warm feelings for animals with whom he was acquainted, it's possible to overstate the case. "Why do we not," asked Sancho of the group, "hunt little birds and bunnies? In that case I would not have torn my coat."

But let us leave aside the question of whatever crimes might have been wrought by little birds and bunnies to deserve a cruel and bloody death by swords. (The pig was blameless also, to be sure.) Other great events need our attention.

As the shadows lengthened in the wood, the peace was rent anew by raucous noise. Cacophony. Bugles and military instruments of every kind: trumpets, drums, and fifes – all at once, together, out of tune. One could not call it music. Suddenly the woods were pandemonium.

Did an army come this way? Fires jumped to life beyond the clearing in the trees. Fires? And then the wood fell silent. The party-goers gaped with pounding hearts.

A post-boy in devil's dress appeared upon a horse. He lifted up a horn and blew one loud and mournful note.

"I am the devil," said the boy, "looking for the knight called Don Quixote. A chariot approaches. It carries Dulcinea del Toboso. With her is the Frenchman Montesinos, who will tell the famous knight how he might remove the lady's spell."

The devil blew his horn again and rode away.

All were astonished, or let us say, all seemed so. The duke and duchess, frozen, stared and waited. Sancho trembled, terrified. His head was emptied now of birds and bunnies.

Quixote was struck dumb with awe. What was this but some sort of dream made flesh? Montesinos would arrive among them? Montesinos? The old man he had met within the cave? Were the things that happened in the Cave of Montesinos real?

No one spoke. The wood was quiet. Silent. Dark. But not for long. The night was pierced by flitting lights, tiny shooting stars among the trees. Shooting stars and then a din to stop the stoutest heart: shots of muskets, human cries of war, drums and horns and bugles, giving way to moaning and to creaking; an oxcart, out of nowhere, came their way.

The cart was drawn by oxen, draped in black, with burning torches fastened to their horns. Upon the cart were demons, so hideous that Sancho Panza had to close his eyes. Upon the cart, upon a chair, there rode a bearded man. His beard was white and fell below his waist. He wore a long, black robe.

"I am the sage Lirandeo," he called out.

The cart rolled on and out of view.

Silence. Then another cart appeared. Another man aboard it called his name.

"I am the sage Alquife, friend of Urganda the Unknowable." His cart rolled by and vanished in the dark.

Another cart, another man; this man large and strong, with a face as cruel as sharpened knives.

"I am the enchanter Arcalaus, enemy of knights." His cart rolled by and disappeared as well.

And then? What next? No fearsome noise, but music. Pretty strains, gentle and harmonious. What now? Did this mean the worst had passed, perhaps? The worst, perhaps, but not the most amazing.

In our time and place, we won't have ever seen a cart such as the one which now came through the wood. It was three times as large as any of the carts that had preceded it: a triumphal chariot, drawn by six brown mules all draped in white. Each mule carried a penitent, a sinner who was paying for his sins. Each sinner held a lighted torch. The chariot bore penitents as well – six perched on either side with lighted torches. And high upon the cart, surrounded by these sinners, sat a nymph – a maiden of such loveliness she was as much a goddess as a girl, clothed in shining veils of gold and silver. And next to her, a massive black-clad figure, enormous and enveloped in a cloak.

This chariot did not pass by. It stopped, and when it did, the music stopped as well. The black-draped figure rose and threw his shrouds apart. Oh, how can one describe a face so gruesome? It was the very face of Death itself. The flesh was gone, and yet the monster could still speak, and did.

"I am Merlin," said the face of Death. "And in the very darkest reaches of the hell that is my home, I heard the weeping voice of Dulcinea. I heard how she was turned from Lady Fair to lowborn wench. I've brought her here, restored for just this moment to her proper form. And I have come to tell you of a remedy. I bring this message to the great Quixote."

Still, no one spoke.

"To disenchant the Lady Dulcinea," said the great magician to Quixote, "your squire Sancho Panza must beat himself, and beat himself upon his very backside. He must do this thing three thousand and three hundred times. His backside must be bare so that he will keenly feel the force of every lash. His backside will sting and vex him sore."

Dear Reader, are you wondering if, reading this last paragraph, you somehow drifted off to sleep and had a dream? Could Dulcinea's fate be solved by comedy? How could such undignified instructions have found their way into our proper tale?

"What has my arse to do with Dulcinea?" So asked Sancho Panza. (Caught off guard, he used the common language of the countryside.) "I will do no such thing."

But Sancho Panza's backside would be beaten, at least if Don Quixote had his way. The knight was every bit as stupefied as any who were in the wood that night, by the evening's many strange events. Still, Don Quixote gave a quick response.

Reaching for his sword, Quixote said, "Sancho Panza, I will tie you to a tree and give you each and every lash myself."

"No!" commanded Merlin. "The squire must complete this task himself. This alone will break the magic spell."

"Well," said Sancho Panza, "then she will forever be enchanted. Why should my backside pay for all her sins? And it's my master who every moment says she is his very life and soul. His knightly rump should feel the whip, instead."

But here the squabbling gentlemen were silenced. The lovely maiden on the cart stood and raised her veil. In haughty tones she thus addressed the squire:

"Oh, wretched squire. Creature with a soul of lead, a heart of wood, guts of stone and granite. You are not asked to jump off some high tower, to take the lives of all your children and your wife. You are not asked to eat the flesh of lizards or of toads. You're only asked to take the sort of punishment that orphan children suffer each and every day. A beating! Do you not see my eyes are wet with tears? My youth is passing by.

"Lash that vast behind of yours, you heartless beast! Release my gentle character and flawless face. And if you will not do these things for my sake, do them for your master, Don Quixote."

The lovely girl fell silent. Her veil slipped down across her perfect face. Silence, once again within the forest, save for the breezes in the leaves in the wake of Dulcinea's words.

"I would like to know where this lady learned the art of asking favors," said Sancho Panza. "She calls me first one foul thing and then another, and tops it off by making her demand. And as for Don Quixote, he says that he will tie me up and beat me. Perhaps these two should learn some plain good manners."

There is no doubt this was a point well taken. There was a standoff in the darkened wood.

It was the duke who settled things. "How can I send to the island you will govern," he asked the squire, "a ruler with as cold a heart as yours? How can I send a governor who will not help a damsel in distress? If you're to be a governor you must agree to rescue Dulcinea."

Why Sancho? Why should he sacrifice his guiltless rump? Why should his hide be offered up to mitigate the sufferings of others?

The world just sometimes seems to ask "Why not?"

The cart began to move away, the flutes to play. As Dulcinea passed the duke and duchess she bowed her head. She curtseyed as she passed by Sancho Panza. Don Quixote, overjoyed, kissed his squire and draped his arms around the poor man's neck, friendly now that his own will had won. The duke and duchess smiled and laughed, delighted with their night of fun and games.

Perhaps you have suspected this: the pageant in the forest was dreamed up by the hosts: the duke and duchess. A page had played the part of Dulcinea. The duke's own butler took the role of Merlin.

They were inventive and industrious, the ducal pair, with no consciences to complicate their sport.

Dawn came. The day ahead would be both calm and clear. Fresh breezes blew. The flowers of the meadows lifted up their heads. The sky was bright; the happy streams flowed shimmering within their banks. Dancing light. A laughing, glinting sky, laughing down upon the waking world.

THE COUNTESS TRIFALDI;
A JOURNEY THROUGH THE AIR

⟨∭⟩

The next day in the garden, the duke and duchess, Don Quixote and the squire were having lunch, when what should meet their ears but pipes and drums – roughly played and coming ever closer.

Sancho Panza instantly was terrified. In this tale, sudden offstage instruments bode ill. Sancho Panza climbed upon the duchess to watch events unfold from her lap.

Two men made their entrance, dressed in black and beating huge black drums. Alongside, was a man who played a fife. Behind them walked a very large companion, draped from tip to toe in great black robes. Across his chest he wore a long curved knife.

He made his way into the luncheon party and dropped down to his knees before the duke, who bid the stranger rise. The stranger rose and lifted up his veil to show his face. He had a beard, so long and thick, it was a freak of nature, as though it had kept growing in the grave.

"My name," he said, "is Trifaldin, squire to the countess called Trifaldi, from whom I bring a message for the knight. She has come to ask a boon of him. She waits outside the gates to make her plea."

"Of, course," the duke replied, "This countess is most welcome in this house." He'd heard of her, the countess called Trifaldi, also called the Dolorous Duenna. (*Dolorous*, is not a word we use much anymore. It means *distressed.*)

The terrible black figure turned to leave the garden, followed by his gloomy band of none-too-gifted, darkly draped musicians.

Now as for Don Quixote, he was, as you might easily predict, delighted to be sent upon a mission. As he had mentioned many times, it wasn't proper that a knight be idle. Sancho, on the other hand – disliking all duennas as he did – was grudging. He was even willing to refuse. (Squires and duennas were famously at odds, like cats and dogs.)

"Duennas," said the squire, "are pests. And worse if they are dolorous as well."

But Don Quixote disagreed. "Duennas can be ladies of high station. If this one is a countess, she must be the duenna of a queen."

The truth is that Quixote was flattered to be sought out for a task. *How wonderful*, he thought. *The maimed and the unfortunate — the pitiful, the lost, the least among us — have now begun to look to me for help.*

Then, out there in the garden, came the sound of instruments again.

Musicians came toward the group, playing fifes and drums. Behind them walked a dozen silent ladies, their faces veiled. The countess made her entrance. She dropped down to her knees before the group.

"Is he here?" the countess cried. "The stainless knight, who's known as Don Quixote?"

"I am Don Quixote," said Quixote, "and I exist to comfort the distressed. Please tell me how you have been made so dolorous."

The Dolorous Duenna called Trifaldi had been the servant of a royal house. The king had died, and she had been entrusted with the care and education of his daughter. The princess was the Princess Antonomasia. The queen was Maguncia, widow of the late King Archipiela. (You won't have to recall these names; don't worry.) They were rulers of the kingdom known as Kandy.

The Princess Antonomasia was beautiful and clever. Noblemen from far and wide had wooed her. It seemed a happy future lay ahead.

But noblemen, despite the name, are not always as noble as they might be. In the throng who sought the maiden's hand, was one who'll make this point, and very well. He was a member of the queen's own court.

Oh, this nobleman had much to recommend him! He was a poet. He was a lively dancer. He was young and he was handsome. He was clever, and an excellent guitarist. Not only that, he was so skilled at building bird cages that he put professionals to shame. (One certainly cannot predict what sorts of talents will turn a young girl's head.) But even such a man as this, with all these many fascinating gifts, will not succeed without a chance to stake his claim. He had to meet the princess all alone.

"He set about securing my allegiance. He weakened me with flattery and trinkets. My heart was softened by his mournful singing; songs that pierced into my soul like thorns. Don Clavijo – this was his name – told me he would marry my fair princess, although this was a promise with no meaning. She was the daughter of a king and queen. He could never marry her. Somehow, though, he managed to persuade me.

"I let him in the chambers of the princess."

Dear Reader, we won't follow Don Clavijo. We'll stay out in the hallway, not daring to guess at goings-on behind the door.

What do we hear? We place our fingers in our ears and hum.

Whatever ways they found to pass the time are their concern. I must, however, write of the results. Before too long, the Princess Antonomasia discovered that she would become a mother.

"There was no time to spare," said the duenna. "The three of us composed a binding document. The nobleman declared, with pen and ink, that he had asked the princess for her hand. The princess wrote that she agreed to marry him. It was a most lopsided match. She was a princess, after all, and he a nobleman of low degree. The queen would not agree to this arrangement. Yet they must wed. We took our contract to the vicar-general. He signed it and the marriage was performed.

"The deed was done. The queen, at last, was told the news and within three short days lay in the ground."

The speaker, the Most Dolorous Duenna, paused to let the tragic tale sink in.

Sancho Panza broke the spell, bringing up a detail he found troubling.

"I suppose that, if they buried her, the queen was dead."

"Of course she was!" Trifaldi said. "In Kandy we do not inter the living."

Indeed, the queen had died of grief (her darling girl had wed below her station), but the story does not stop here at her grave.

The moment that her tomb was closed, a giant on a wooden horse appeared.

The giant was Malambrano, an enchanter and a cousin to the queen. He cast a spell. The princess Antonomasia was turned into a monkey made of brass. The nobleman became a crocodile, fashioned of some odd, unheard-of metal. Between them stood a column with these words:

> *These two foolish lovers will stay just as they are, until the great Malambrano does battle with Quixote of La Mancha. For him alone the Fates reserve this mission.*

What's more, the magic giant did not stop at punishing the princess and her husband, Don Clavijo. He insisted each and every last duenna of Antonomasia's palace would pay a price as well. He would make these women outcasts, beyond the love and pity of any who would look upon their faces.

In the garden of the duke's estate, the duennas of Trifaldi lifted up their veils to show the outcome of the giant's curse.

They wore beards! This was the giant's vulgar retribution.

"Could there have been no other way of punishing these duennas than by bearding them?" Sancho asked the question of the group. "Perhaps, instead, the giant could have taken off some portion of their noses. Perhaps he could have taken off the half above the middle, even if their speech would be unclear." This was the stingy mercy the squire thought was fitting for duennas.

"I will do whatever must be done to lift the giant's spell," said Don Quixote.

"Our kingdom," said the Dolorous Duenna, "is five thousand leagues away, give or take a couple thousand leagues." She had instructions ready for the knight. "It's far from here but you can be transported at such a speed you'll feel that you've been carried off by devils. The giant who imposed this curse will send a horse to fetch you from the garden – a wooden horse whose name is Clavileno, created by the great magician, Merlin. This horse, as he is wooden, does not eat or sleep, and moves along so smoothly through the air that you could hold a cup of water in your hand and never spill a drop. You'll guide him with a wooden peg. There is a peg protruding from his head. By turning it, you can make the horse fly high in the sky or low and brushing close against the ground. But a middle course in altitude would be best, as in all other things. The horse is on its way. It should arrive here at the palace soon."

"How many people can this horse take on its back?" asked Sancho.

"Two," said the duenna. "One in the saddle up in front. Another hanging on behind, unsaddled."

"Well, truly this invention does sound wonderful," said Sancho, "but I will tell you here and now, if you think I'm joining Don Quixote on this trip, you'll find that you are very much mistaken. There will be figs on thistles before you'll find me riding for five thousand leagues, unsaddled on a wooden horse's flanks. I can hardly stay on Dapple, my own donkey, and Dapple wears a saddle soft as silk. No, my master will take on this task alone. I will stay and give myself my beating."

"Sancho," said Quixote to the group, "will do my bidding when the horse appears. We will go forth upon this wooden horse and I will slice Malambrano's head from off his neck."

Sancho, for the moment, was ignored.

As darkness fell, the horse arrived, carried to the garden by two men. The men were dressed in ivy leaves. The book describes these characters as "wild men."

"Let he who has the courage, climb upon the horse," said one.

"Well, then I am excused," said Sancho Panza.

"The squire," said a wild man, "will ride here on the back. The knight will take the saddle up in front."

Had no one heard the squire speak? Sancho Panza had said he would not go.

"The horse will take the knight and squire to Kandy," said a wild man. "The giant waits. We have blindfolds for the travelers, so they won't be dizzy on the trip."

At this, the wild men in leaves began to dance. They leaped and twirled and swooped and pounced and sprang and skipped and thus they made their way out of the garden.

"I will not go," said Sancho once again. "My master needs another squire to take along. I'm not some witch who likes to go off flying. What happens if our plans do not turn out? What if the wooden horse should tire? Of if the giant is extremely angry? No, I will stay here and become a governor. I hope these bearded ladies will forgive me."

This final time, the duke stepped in. Of course, he understood the squire's worries. He spoke to Sancho Panza, man-to-man, as one man of the world does to another.

"You know" he said, "positions such as governor are almost always given for a handsome bribe. You're wise enough to know this, I am sure. I tell you, you must go with Don Quixote. Your island will be here when you return, the islanders all clamoring to greet you."

And so the squire who wished to be a governor, clambered onto the wooden horse's rear. Don Quixote climbed into the saddle. They both put on their blindfolds and Don Quixote grasped the horse's steering peg to make the wooden beast rise from the ground. The people in the garden waved them off and gasped and squealed and marveled at the marvelous departure of our heroes.

"God be with you, noble knight," called one.

"God guide you, loyal squire."

"We watch with admiration as you rise up into the sky!"

"Godspeed!"

Sancho held on tight, so tight around Quixote's waist that finally the knight had to admonish him. Sancho was afraid, despite the fact that judging from the voices of the crowd below – and this he pointed out – it was as though they hadn't moved an inch.

"This is to be expected," said Quixote. "We are on a magic horse. We can't expect the normal course of things. The voices on the ground seem to be much closer than they are. In circumstances such as this, you might hear things a thousand miles away, as though they have been whispered in your ear."

And just as the duenna had predicted, the ride upon the horse was smooth as glass – so smooth, it seemed again, as if the horse had stayed upon the ground among the trees.

As, in fact, it had.

The story of the Dolorous Duenna, the giant, and the wooden horse was more chicanery, of course, dreamed up by Their Highnesses to pass the time. (Highnesses have lots of time to spare.) The party guests – all privy to this secret – cooperated at each stage, now pumping bellows at our heroes' faces to replicate the feel of rushing wind.

"There's such a wind upon my face," said Sancho, "it's just as if we two are blown by bellows."

A wind as strong as bellows. Don Quixote, up in front, explained to Sancho what such winds implied.

"We have reached the second region of the air," he called above the gusting wind. "This is where the snow and hail are made. Above us is another region, which is the source of thunderbolts and lightning. And farther up there is the realm of fire, to which we must not go, lest we be roasted."

The wily duke and duchess had prepared a torch. They lit it now and held it up.

"We're in the place of fire now," called Sancho. "I'm almost sure my beard is singed." (Perhaps it felt no different than if someone had held a torch next to his face.)

On went Don Quixote and his squire, rushing through the air and staying still. The duke and duchess and their band of tricksters delighted at the talk between our heroes. They were so brave – the knight and squire – not knowing that they faced no kind of danger.

But all good things must end. When the party in the garden had wrung whatever joy they could from making playthings of their trusting friends, they set the wooden horse's tail alight, setting off explosives that were hidden in its rear. The horse was thrown into the air, its riders tossed onto the ground, scorched and singed and most of all, bewildered.

Where were they? Quixote and his squire took their blindfolds off. They were somehow in the garden of the duke. Was there a giant? There was not. Here was instead the duke and all his party scattered on the ground like lifeless puppets. The duennas, they discovered, had departed.

The ducal party seemed to be unconscious. The knight and squire staggered to their feet.

At the garden's edge there was a lance, thrust in the ground. From the lance there hung a sort of letter. The pair picked through the sleeping guests to read it.

On a parchment hung from silken cords was written this:

> *The great Knight Don Quixote has concluded his adventure on behalf of the Duenna of Trifaldi. He has accomplished this merely by attempting it. The giant Malambrano is satisfied. The duennas are all free and clean of face. Antonomasia and her new husband are now restored to human form. Dulcinea will be disenchanted once the squire's thrashings are complete.*

The duke awoke and yawned, stretching both his arms, as people do when they've been feigning sleep. The others in the garden came to life, and once they all had seemed to be revived, Sancho told the duchess the many thrilling details of the trip.

"I sensed us rising through the air," he said, "and though my master had forbidden me to take a look, I moved aside my blindfold, for I'm the sort of man who's very curious. From where we flew, the earth below us looked no bigger than a mustard seed, the men upon it no larger than mere hazelnuts."

"But Sancho," said the duchess, "hazelnuts are bigger than are mustard seeds. How can the people of the earth have seemed like hazelnuts when the earth was tiny like a mustard seed?"

"Perhaps I saw it from the side," said Sancho.

"But how does that explain it?" asked the duchess.

"Your Ladyship should understand that we were borne above the earth by magic. By magic I could see all I describe. And if you don't believe me, you'll not believe what took place next. Up there in the heavens I peeked again, and saw that we were flying past the stars that people in your part of Spain call Seven Sisters. In my part of Spain they are called the Seven Goats. Well, I was a goatherd as a boy, and love those little beasts. And so it was that up there in the sky, I could not resist their company. I slipped off the horse's back to play with them. While I played, the horse stood still to wait. The goats were just as pretty as petunias."

"And while you were cavorting with the goats," the duke inquired, "how was Don Quixote occupied?"

Quixote had been silent for this foolishness. He now spoke up.

"My squire's either lying or he's dreaming," said the knight. "I never moved my blindfold. I didn't see the sky or earth. But though I felt the coursing of the wind upon my face, and though I felt the heat of fire, I do not think we flew up high enough to reach the Seven Goats."

"Saw them I did," said Sancho Panza, "and I recall exactly what they looked like. Two of the goats were green and two were blue and two were red and one was all these colors mixed. Of course, one would expect that goats up in the heavens would not be like the ones down here on earth. None of this is very strange to me."

Don Quixote leaned in close and whispered in the squire's ear: "Sancho, since you tell us that we are to take your word for all of this, I want you to believe that all I told you of the Cave of Montesinos did take place. And of this matter I will say no more."

So ended the adventure of the magic horse, a tale the duke and duchess talked about and laughed about, delighting in their cleverness, for years to come.

SANCHO PANZA BECOMES A GOVERNOR;
A LOVE SONG FOR QUIXOTE;
SANCHO PANZA, WISE AND GOOD.

The duke was as good as his word. On the day that followed the flight upon the wooden horse, the duke told Sancho Panza he must pack his bags. He was to be a governor and the islanders that he would rule were yearning to be led "as eager as for rain during a drought."

It was good news, of course – the elevation Sancho had been counting on all through his days of hunger, thirst, and worry, through all his many beatings, shocks, and tight escapes, through many nights of sleeping on the forest floor, subject to his master's endless chatter – it was good news.

But Sancho Panza had some reservations when the moment came. You see, the squire had seen with his own eyes, from atop the horse high in the sky, just how small and insignificant is humankind. He had become, the day before, a little wiser. The earth was nothing greater than a mustard seed – humans, merely hazelnuts astride it.

"What grandeur can there be in holding office over men no larger than mere hazelnuts?" So asked the thoughtful squire of the duke.

The duke, who was no stranger to deep thinking, assured the squire that once he'd had a taste of giving orders, he "would eat his hands off to have more, so sweet it is to give commands and be obeyed."

The Duke sent Sancho Panza to the tailor. He would need a special set of clothes. Great men of government, of law, of the university, and military, for example, must have fancy dress to match their station. An outfit was selected – something of a captain's suit with a touch of lawyer's garb as well, as befits a man of action and of judgment.

When Don Quixote heard the news – that Sancho would be leaving for his island – he knew he had a role to play in readying the squire for his station. And knew as well, as you will see, that true friends, if they are true friends, don't mince their words. "As far as I'm concerned," Quixote said, "you are – I tell the truth – a sort of dimwit. And yet, you are embarking on great things."

He took his squire by the hand, led him to his room, and closed the door. He offered up his counsel on how the squire should behave in office. Dear Reader, I include it here, in case you're ever called upon to govern:

You must fear God, for in the fear of God, lies wisdom.

You must remember who you are. Knowing who you are is very difficult, but it will stop you from becoming puffed up (like the frog who thought himself the equal of an ox).

Glory in your humble stock. Blood is inherited, but virtue is acquired and has a value that blood does not.

If you take your wife to govern with you, see that she behaves in ways that do you credit.

Never make your whims the law.

Let a poor man's pleas move you to compassion, but not to greater justice than that you give the rich.

Apply leniency whenever possible.

When you judge a case involving an enemy, put your own grievances aside.

When a beautiful woman appears before you, turn your eyes away from her, and ponder soberly the merits of her plea.

If you are going to punish a criminal with deeds, do not also punish him with words.

Think of any culprit who comes before you as deserving pity. Be compassionate if you can. All God's attributes are excellent, but mercy is more excellent than justice.

Be clean and cut your fingernails.

Do not go about with your clothes loose and flapping.

When you give food and clothing to your servants, make sure they are practical and not showy, and give these things to the poor as well.

Do not eat garlic and onions, else people will know you are a peasant.

Walk calmly. Speak carefully, but don't go listening to the sound of your own voice.

Eat a small lunch and a smaller dinner.

Don't drink too much wine.

Chew on both sides of your mouth.

Don't eructate.

"What do you mean, *eructate*?" asked the squire

"The vulgar term for this is belch," Quixote said. "*Belch* is a word you should not use. Don't say this word. Use the word *eructate*."

The knight went on.

When you ride your horse, be neither too upright nor too relaxed upon the saddle.

Do not sleep too much.

Do not enter into any arguments which compare the pedigrees of one family against another. The family you deem lower will hate you, and the family you deem superior will be too lofty to reward you.

Wear a long coat. Do not wear short breeches. They are not suitable for knights and governors.

᠃᠃᠃

That very afternoon Sancho set off in the company of servants, dressed up like a man of deed and thought. Dapple,

Sancho Panza's ass, was draped in silk. On this day he would not bear a load.

Don Quixote's heart was very heavy. For all that he was expert at picking out his squire's many failings, for all that he felt free to point them out (and what are true friends for?), Don Quixote felt the squire's loss most keenly. In point of fact, if he could have found a way to rob the squire of his great good fortune – if Sancho could have been prevented from departing – Don Quixote quickly would have seen it done. (We will not blame Quixote. Friendship's often quite a mix of good and bad; people will say otherwise, but love will rarely render us unselfish.)

Farewells said and waving done, Don Quixote retreated to his rooms to be alone. He asked the household staff to leave him be. By the light of two wax candles he undressed. And then he blew the candles out and opened up the window for some air. The cool night drifted in.

Gone was Sancho Panza to his destiny. Gone was Sancho Panza to that great abyss that people call the future. And Don Quixote, standing at the window, faced his own abyss, but now alone.

But what was this? Above the hush of breeze and leaves, he heard a voice.

"Don't insist I sing."

It was a maiden's voice, lifting to the window from the garden. "Ever since the stranger came, I cannot sing. I only weep. Besides, the knight's asleep. He will not hear me."

"He is awake." Another maiden spoke. "I believe I heard him at his window."

"I cannot sing," the girl replied. "I can't reveal the secrets of my heart. I'll be considered flighty by anyone who does not know the awful crushing force of love."

As Don Quixote listened, the lady played her harp and then unleashed her longings in a song. She loved him. (She could not sing? She could!) She loved the knight who listened at the window.

Oh, Don Quixote'd faced this test before. This lady in the garden was not the first to love the knight whose heart and soul were sworn to Dulcinea.

In the window, Don Quixote sneezed. He was a gentleman and he chose this way to let the maidens know that he was wide awake. Down below, the lady sang, knowing that he heard her every word. (Bold as brass she was, if you ask me.)

For Dulcinea, I am fluffy pastry, thought the knight. *For every other woman I am flint. For Dulcinea I am sweetest honey. For any other woman I am cactus.*

He closed the window, lay down on the bed.

Earlier he asked that he be left alone, and now the time has come to grant his wish.

⚬〰〰〰⚬

The town of Baratario was renamed Baratavia – a city of five thousand souls, who, as the Duke had promised, were overjoyed, it seemed, to meet their ruler. The city council came to meet the squire at the city gates. Bells were rung, hands shaken, and backs slapped. Cheers went up. Sancho and his retinue were taken to the parish church for formal ceremonies and rejoicing.

A brief and silly ceremony followed. (The historian will not stoop to describe it. He will only say that it was ludicrous.) The townsfolk had been told what roles to play. Sancho was presented with the city keys, and then – no time to waste – was taken from the church into the courtroom.

It was the custom, in these parts, to set before new governors some problems. How their brand-new leader solved the puzzles would let his subjects know what to expect.

Sancho took his seat on the judge's bench. (Great men, you see, need special chairs, high up so that they peer down on the common folk.)

Two men came in and stood before the governor. One was a farmer, the other one a tailor. Their disagreement, as the tailor summed it up, was this:

"Yesterday this farmer came into my shop. He brought a piece of cloth and asked if it was large enough to make a hood. I said it was. Now, customers will sometimes worry that tailors will not tell them when the piece of cloth they've brought is much too big. They worry that the tailor plans to keep the scraps for other jobs. And so this farmer asked me if the cloth he'd brought might be big enough to make two hoods. This way he could be sure that every tiny bit of cloth was used. I said I thought there was enough for two.

"And then this farmer asked me if I could make three hoods, instead of two. Had he brought me cloth enough for three?

"I said he had.

"Well, maybe, asked the farmer, I could make four or five?

"I said I could, and this I did. This afternoon he came to get the hoods. I made five hoods, but now he will not pay me."

"Is this all true?" asked Sancho of the farmer.

"It is," the farmer said, "but have the tailor show you what he made."

"Gladly," said the tailor. He brought his hand from underneath his cape. Upon each finger was a tiny hood. He'd made five hoods, exactly as he'd promised. The farmer hadn't specified the size.

"What's needed for this verdict is mere common sense," said Sancho. "The tailor will not get his pay. The hoods are much too small to be of use. The farmer will give up his cloth because the tailor did fulfill his order. The hoods will be donated to the prison for the prisoners." (Perhaps he thought that prisoners, with all the extra time at their disposal, might come up with a use for tiny hoods.)

Thus ended the first case before the governor.

Two old men were next in line. One of them was walking with a cane.

The man who had no cane explained the case:

"I lent this man some money and recently I asked him to repay me. But he denies he ever borrowed money, and further says that if he did, he's paid it back. He's slippery and doesn't keep his story straight. Governor, I ask you this. Have him swear before you that he's paid me back. If he'll do so, I will take him at his word. I know I do not trust him, but I know as well he is God-fearing. I do not think that he will swear to lies."

"What do you say to this?" asked Sancho of the man who held the cane.

"I will admit the fellow lent me money," said the man. "But I'm prepared to swear I've paid him back."

All were agreed. Sancho took his mighty staff – a handsome object topped off with a cross – and lowered it, so that the man who was to swear could touch it as he made his oath. The man who'd borrowed money passed his cane over to the lender, to free his hands, to place them on the cross. He placed his hands upon the cross and swore that he'd returned the borrowed money.

And in this way, the matter seemed concluded. Once the borrower had sworn his oath, the lender said he would accept his word. The borrower took back his cane and left the hall.

But Sancho could not shake some nagging instinct.

He asked that the defendant with the cane return, and when he was brought back, Sancho said his cane should be cracked open. This was done. Hidden in the cane was the very sum that its owner owed.

Now, how had Sancho Panza known to look inside the cane?

Do you recall, before he'd sworn his oath the borrower had given up his cane to the other man to hold? And that he'd had it back the very moment that the oath was done? For just the very moment of the swearing of the oath, he had, as he had sworn, returned the money. The money had been hidden in the cane. The owner of the cane had found a way to tell the truth while lying.

Now the lender had his money back. He counted it and rolled it up and left.

There was one further case for Sancho Panza. It was a rather sordid disagreement. Perhaps it's best we not go into detail. Suffice it that I tell you this: a pig herder had wooed a local lady. He'd met her just that afternoon and courted her and won her in a roadside ditch. But when their hasty interlude had ended, they had a lovers' spat, as lovers will. (Romance is frail. Sometimes it does not last.) It seems the damsel had expected payment.

Let's tiptoe from the courtroom while they argue. Don Quixote waits for our return.

CATS AND BELLS; A DISAPPOINTING
DINNER; A LETTER FROM THE DUKE;
A VISIT LATE AT NIGHT.

꧁꧂

In the castle of the duke, Don Quixote lay upon his bed. Benengeli tells us that Quixote's thoughts were like a plague of fleas. They came with him to bed and would not let him have a moment's rest. He was troubled by the singing of the maiden. The night wore on. Quixote did not sleep.

When morning came, Don Quixote took his sword, gathered up his rosary, and set out through the palace to bid good morning to the duke and duchess.

But the ladies from the garden lay in wait.

The lovesick singer Don Quixote had heard the night before was called Altisidora. Now we meet her by the light of day. She and her companion awaited Don Quixote in the halls.

When Don Quixote showed his face, Altisidora fainted dead away. Or, let's just say she closed her eyes and fell. As

Don Quixote, pop-eyed with astonishment, looked on, Altisidora's friend untied the maiden's bodice strings to give her air.

Poor Don Quixote, conqueror of monsters and of maidens. Monsters he would joyously destroy. Maidens were his unintended victims, laid waste by nothing that he meant to do, brought to their undoing by his charms.

As Altisidora swooned, unlaced before him, Don Quixote told her worried fellow that he'd seen this kind of thing before, and knew what he could do to set things right.

"I will ease the lovesick lady's grief. In circumstances such as these, undeceiving is the only cure. She must give up hope that she can win my heart."

That night he'd sing a song, he said, to tell the girl, as gently as he could, the reasons why their love could never be. Could he be provided with a lute?

As soon as Don Quixote'd left the passageway, Altisidora jumped to her feet. And when the coast was clear, she and her companion made haste to bring their story to his hosts. The duke and duchess clapped their hands and chuckled. This was a brand-new opportunity for playing tricks. (This pair was rendered infantile by privilege. As you go through life you'll see this happen.)

When evening came, Don Quixote tuned his lute and opened wide the window to the garden. He cleared his throat and spat and in a singing voice, both none-too-good and none-too-poor, embarked upon the story of his iron-clad devotion to his Lady Fair.

He sang, and then he paused for breath. He heard the sounds of movement in the garden. Yes. Someone listened quietly below.

But what was this? Suddenly another sound. Of bells? Of cats? It came not from below, but from above.

One hundred goat bells tied to rope were lowered from the balcony above him. And to the rope was tied a sack of cats, each cat with tiny bells tied to his tail. Noise. Confusion. Panic. The bells and cats were lowered down and ended their descent outside the window.

It's possible the masterminds behind this plan had not intended all the things that happened next. The book reports the duke and duchess were every bit as shocked as Don Quixote, when the cats escaped their bag and found their way in through Quixote's window.

Once inside Quixote's room, the cats were helter-skelter with confusion, knocking out the candles, scrambling and screeching in the dark, terror-stricken, chased by bells. Quixote flailed, not seeing his assailants (not knowing they were merely kitty cats). He found his sword and swung it at the frenzied beasts. "Away with you, enchanters!" cried the knight. "I am Don Quixote of La Mancha, against whom all your evil aims are powerless."

So cried Quixote to his little foes. But one of these, perhaps more frightened than the others (or more brave), fell with claws outstretched upon Quixote's face and held on tight.

It was Don Quixote's screaming at this injury that finally had the duke and duchess burst through his door to stop their prank.

But Quixote would not let himself be rescued.

"No one must pull my enemy from off my face! I will fight him man-to-man. He will taste the wrath of Don Quixote."

Even now, he did not seem to know he fought a cat. And, by the way, this was a cat who seemed to share the knight's devotion to chivalric code: death was to be prized over defeat. This cat would not be vanquished. Back and forth, across the room, Quixote and his adversary struggled. Finally, the duke was able to dislodge the beast, who beat a hasty exit out the window. (Perhaps this mission wasn't meant for him.)

The bedroom was a shambles. Don Quixote's nose was torn and bleeding. The duke and duchess sent for healing oil. And whom did they assign to tend his wounds? Altisidora, who tended to Quixote's wounds but did inflict some damage of her own. She battered him with sharp recriminations.

"These mishaps have befallen you, stone-hearted knight, for the sin of your cold-heartedness. May Dulcinea never be set free."

Don Quixote stayed in bed five days.

We'll leave him to recuperate. The author of this history sweeps his wand across the stage. He shows us Sancho Panza, who, as we watch, is going in to dinner.

⟨⟫⟩

If you were Sancho Panza (and you know him very well by now), what do you think might be the thing you'd most enjoy if you were made a governor? Would it be the opportunity to improve the lives of people whom you ruled? Would it be the place you're given at the very heart of great events? Would it be the chance to test your gifts at leadership – to meet the many challenges that come along? Or would it be, by any chance, the food?

Let's not assume that Sancho was unmoved by lofty aims in taking office, but let's admit (we might as well) he was devoted foremost to his dinner.

On that first day when judgments were completed, the governor was taken to a palace. A great hall had been readied for his meal. The table, vast and elegant, was laid with just one setting at the end. Pots and plates were placed along the table's length, hidden under spotless squares of linen.

Music played. Four pages held out water for the governor to wash his hands, and Sancho took his place to start his meal.

A personage appeared. He seemed to be a man of great importance. He held a whalebone pointer and motioned that the feast was to begin. A servant pulled a cloth aside. A page said grace. Another tied a frilly bib at Sancho's neck. A steward came forth with a plate of fruit.

Sancho took a bite, and was no doubt preparing for another, when the personage beside him lifted up the whalebone rod and tapped it gently on the plate of fruit. A steward stepped up quickly and took the dish away, and brought a plate of meat to take its place.

Sancho took a bite of meat and would have had another, but once again the whalebone pointer dropped to tap the plate from which he ate. The plate was carried off. Sancho Panza looked around, bewildered.

"I am a doctor," said the man who manned the whalebone rod. "It is my duty to protect your health. I must decide what and in what quantities you eat. The fruit that you were served seemed to me to be too moist. And it was my decision that the second dish you took was far too hot. It had spices that could increase your thirst and might encourage you to drink water in such quantities that you would destroy the balance of the humors."

Sancho Panza pointed down the table to a ravishing display of roasted partridge.

"Those do not look spicy."

"You'll not eat those," the doctor said, "as long as there is breath within my body. All excess is dangerous, and this applies especially to the partridge."

"Then, perhaps you'll look about the table and find the dishes that are safe to eat. And do so quickly, if you would, before I drop down dead from sheer starvation."

The doctor looked about among the dishes.

"You must not eat the rabbit stew. I can't condone the meat of furry animals. And if the veal had not been served in hearty sauce, I might have found a way to let you try it. As it is, I know it will not do. As for the stew, I simply cannot let you eat a meal of such variety. Who knows what the proportions are? I cannot guess what dangers you might face. I believe what I will recommend is wafers for your meal, and maybe just a little slice of jelly."

All this was too much for Sancho Panza. He was an even-tempered sort, but even even-tempered sorts have limits. Sancho leaned back in his chair and bellowed.

"Take this doctor from my sight at once! If he stays, I tell you I will cudgel him and beat him off the island. Remove him, or I will take this chair that I am sitting on and smash it on his head. And now I'd like my dinner, and if I do not have it, I will not be your governor for all the world."

The doctor fled the banquet hall. As he hurried from the room he passed another man who hurried in. A messenger – sweating, panting, overwrought – rushed toward the table.

He had an urgent letter from the duke. He placed the letter into Sancho's hands.

Now, the reader must be let in on a secret. Sancho Panza was a man of many talents; the book reveals them with each passing page. But Sancho could not read or write and had no wish to have his subjects know this.

"Which one of you," asked Sancho, "is my secretary?"

One of the servants said that it was he.

"Read the letter to me. It is beneath my station to take such humble tasks upon myself."

The servant read the letter to the governor.

> *To Senor Don Sancho Panza.*
> *It has come to my notice that there are enemies of your island who plan to attack you in one night's time. You must stay awake, so as not to be caught off-guard. Also, do not eat anything you are given, lest the food be poisoned. I will certainly provide assistance if you are in difficulties and know I can count on you to behave as is suitable to someone in your high office.*
> *Your friend,*
> *The Duke.*

Despite the Duke's instructions in the letter, Sancho Panza knew what he must do. He would need strength in order to defend his little island. He must eat. "I'll have a hunk of bread and I would like some grapes. Poison can't be hidden inside grapes."

"Now," he said, "I want that doctor with the whalebone stick locked up. Without delay. Find him. Put him in the dungeon. I think he means to kill me through starvation. If any man endangers me it's he!"

And to his secretary he said this: "You must write the duke a letter. Tell him that his orders will be followed.

"Where is the bread?" he asked. "Where are the grapes?

"Tell the duke as well, that I kiss the hands of the Lady Duchess and while you write of kissing hands, include those of the knight they call Quixote. I am his grateful servant. Write that down. Kiss the hands. Grateful servant. Add what you like. Now bring the food!"

⚬⚬⚬

We will not leave the island – not when there is danger to be faced. But we will turn our gaze to Don Quixote. We see him in the distance in his rooms where he's been lying on his bed for days. We see him late at night, covered in his bandages and quilts, brought low by cats and bells.

We hear the scuffle of a key. The bedroom door creaks open. Don Quixote listens, lying still.

Oh, Don Quixote knew just who this was. It was the lovesick girl, Altisidora. But, this time, as so often, he was wrong.

It was instead, the duchess' duenna.

It was the haughty character who, on the day our heroes had arrived, told Sancho that duennas don't tend donkeys. On this night however, it was another version of the lady. This version was a gentler soul. She'd come to ask Quixote for a favor. (Wanting things makes people rather sweet.)

Truth to tell, Quixote only listened to the lady with one ear. He was bashful in his nightclothes and suspicious of the lady's true intent. She was a woman, after all – not made of bronze. If young girls lost their hearts to him, then why not she?

Don Quixote listened in his bed, bound up in his bandages and bedspreads. Modestly he tucked his blankets tight beneath his chin.

The duenna took her place beside Quixote's bed and, as she spoke, somehow kept her passions in control. She told Quixote of her treasured daughter, a model of most everything a girl could hope to be. "She sings just like a lark," said the duenna. "She dances faster than a thought. She writes just like a schoolmaster, and her arithmetic! Well, no one can compare. On top of all these blessings she is beautiful."

A pretty singing maiden who danced at lightening speed and knew her sums? How, you ask, could trouble rear its head?

Thus: her daughter had succumbed to a romance. The gentleman had then refused to marry her. And so, said the duenna, she'd come to beg Quixote to find some way to force this man: this dog, this cad, this low born lying scoundrel, this knave, this louse, this bum, this outright bounder to take her daughter's hand in holy wedlock.

"The truth is that my daughter is much finer than any other lady in this court. She certainly outshines Altisidora, who is of common stock and carries, let's admit, a bit of reek. And even our great lady – our own duchess – has most unpleasant aspects to her person."

"The duchess?" asked Quixote. Perhaps the knight had heard her incorrectly. Did she suggest the duchess was imperfect?

"The duchess," said the duenna. "The duchess has two drainage holes cut in her legs, through which her toxic fluids are released."

Drainage holes? Good God! Suddenly, the chamber doors burst open. The candles failed. Crashing. Smashing furniture. The duchess' duenna was attacked. Don Quixote stayed in bed. Modesty prevented him from rising. Close by in the darkened room, the duenna took a paddling with a slipper. Some cruel intruder spanked her with a shoe! The knight was next, chased from underneath his sheets and pinched a hundred times by something or by someone he could not see.

⟨∞⟩

The author moves his wand again and we return our sights to Sancho Panza. This dinnertime was better than the last.

We turn back to the governor and find that he's remembered Don Quixote's counsel. Mercy is more excellent than justice. Sancho had the personage who manned the whalebone pointer be set free. The governor had changed his mind.

The doctor showed his gratitude by granting Sancho Panza an enormous feast: cold meat served with onions, swimming in a pool of oil with rotting calf's feet for an extra treat. Sancho Panza ate with gusto. The governor was not a picky eater.

Then, with dinner over, his belly filled, Sancho Panza gathered up his retinue and set out on a walk to meet his subjects. He strolled along the city streets, finely dressed, accepting compliments and tributes, and solving problems when the need arose.

⟨∞⟩

The author moves his wand again and indicates the palace of the duke to show us who had breached Quixote's bedroom door and had brought on such chaos in the dark. It was Altisidora and the duchess. They had listened at the keyhole as the duchess' duenna told her tale. They were outraged that the lady's toxic drainage holes had been discussed. No lady likes her leakage made so public – whether she be a duchess or a drudge.

Teresa Learns Her Husband is a Governor; A Duenna's Plea; Attack by Night.

⟨ⱥ⟩

Outside the duke's estate, we look on as the front gates slowly open. A page comes out; in his bag are letters from the duchess. We see him take the road toward La Mancha.

The duchess had bounced back from her indignity and she had conjured up a bit of fun. Early in her friendship with the squire, the duchess had encouraged him to send a message to his wife. He'd done so, dictated a letter word for word, but the duchess had not sent the note until this day. The page we see is carrying the letter in his bag, and with it is another, from the duchess to Teresa Panza.

The page, arriving in La Mancha, came upon a group of girls. He asked them where to find the squire's wife. Coincidence! Sancho's daughter was among the girls. Sanchica, messy and bare-legged – running, jumping, shouting with good cheer – led the page directly to her mother.

Teresa, heavy, coarse and friendly, and every bit a proper squire's wife, was more than eager for her husband's news. The stranger read the letters to the ladies.

Sancho's letter started by assuring his fine wife that their donkey was in excellent good health. (Dapple sent his very best regards.) And there was more! Teresa would be thrilled. Sancho would be very soon a governor! Their dreams were coming true. If all went well, he told his wife, there was a chance he'd send for her to join him! (Such a doting husband! Lucky wife!)

The letter from the duchess was more recent. Sancho was a governor already! By all accounts he was a great success. The duchess sent along her warmest wishes and a coral rosary for saying prayers. And she enclosed a hunting coat of worsted wool (slightly torn). But best of all, the duchess wrote that she would find a husband for Sanchica.

Oh, dizzy was Teresa at the news. She sent Sanchica off to find Quixote's friends. She would show this letter to the priest and Bachelor and wave it in their smug and doubting faces. They had thought that Sancho was deluded; he'd never rule an island. How wonderful to see them eat their words.

The page who brought the letter had brought writing instruments as well and took them out to write Teresa's answers. We will read them later in the tale.

But now, back to the island of Baratavia.

Sancho's breakfast on this day was candied fruit. The doctor, a man of strong convictions, explained (brave soul) that small meals make for sharper minds. Reinforced by candied fruits, Sancho Panza took the bench that day to govern.

A stranger came into the court.

"This case is very difficult," the stranger said. "There is a great estate and this estate is made up of two parts. A river cuts the great estate in half, and so there is a bridge across the river.

"At one end of the bridge there is a gallows. And on the bridge there is a tiny courthouse, only large enough to seat four judges. The judges spend their days there to enforce a law which reads as follows: (I will quote directly.)

> *Anyone who wants to cross this bridge must swear to where he's going and must divulge the purpose of his trip. If he tells the truth, he will be free to cross. If he lies, then he will die by hanging.*

"Many people use this bridge," the stranger said. "They state where they are going and give the reason for their trip. In general things runs smoothly. There's never been a problem in the past.

"This morning, though, a traveler arrived with a case that has the judges stymied.

"'My purpose,' said the traveler, 'is to die by hanging from the gallows.'

"If the man is judged to tell the truth, he must be allowed to cross the bridge. Therefore, if he tells the truth, he must not hang. In which case, he will not have met his death upon the gallows, which makes him, then, a liar. And if he is a liar, he must hang.

"If he is to climb up to the gallows and be hanged, he will have told the truth about the purpose of his trip, and should have passed, unharmed, across the bridge.

"The judges have sent me here to ask you for an answer. They simply can't decide what they should do."

"Tell the story once again," said Sancho. "I'm a bit dull-witted, I'm afraid."

The stranger told the tale again. (And you might want to read it over, too. One needn't be dull-witted to find the stranger's tale a bit confusing.)

Sancho gave the matter thought. "It seems to me that the judges should allow," he said, "one half of the man who told the truth, to cross the bridge in safety and survive. But they should put to death by hanging, the other half. The half who tells the lie should die for lying."

But Sancho Panza's answer had a flaw. (Can you pick it out? Stop reading for a moment and reflect.)

"This can't be done," the stranger said. "If we divide the man in half then he will die. The half that told the truth would be punished with the half that lied."

"Yes, I see," said Sancho. He thought some more. Considered. "The problem is, it's every bit as reasonable to kill this man as it is to spare him. Therefore I decree that he go free. And here is why. Mercy is more excellent than justice. Doing good is always to be preferred to doing harm. According to the great knight Don Quixote, when there are doubts, one should always take the path of mercy."

It was, we can agree, a brilliant judgment – consulting not the head alone, but taking in the wisdom of the heart. A testament, perhaps, to candied fruit, and to the counsel of the great Quixote.

His morning's work completed, Sancho judged that it was time for lunch. The doctor with the whalebone rod said that their great governor should eat his fill.

Thus fortified, with lunch complete, Sancho Panza went about the making of assorted laws:

Wine could be imported from any region. Anyone discovered watering the wine, or falsifying documents concerning wine, must die; the price of footwear must come down; the rates for servants' wages must be fixed; there must be heavy punishments for singing loudly in the streets; blind men must not sing of miracles unless those miracles were proven true; there was to be a constable whose job would be to find out if the poor who begged along the streets were really poor, or merely feigning poverty for gain.

These laws were thought so useful and fair-minded that they are still in place this very day.

And now we are required at the duke's estate.

⟡⟡⟡

At the palace of the duke, Don Quixote was becoming restless. It had always been his plan to go to Saragossa for the jousting. It seemed to Don Quixote that jousting was a better way for knights to pass their days than lolling in great rooms adorned with tapestries, sleeping on fine sheets with feather pillows, and dining on exotic treats at every meal. At the palace were no needy to be comforted, no beasts to slay, no orphans to defend. He had no earthly reason to remain.

He made his way along the castle's corridors (encountering no needy and no beasts, no orphans and no damsels and no monsters), and found the duke and duchess in a splendid hall. He truly was about to take his leave of them, when fresh events unfolded to prevent him. The doorway to the splendid hall flew open. (Doors fly open often in this tale. Things come crashing through the trees.) Two women dressed in black came rushing forward. One lay down and kissed Quixote's feet, crying out with heartsick moans and sobbing.

At Don Quixote's gentlemanly urging, the weeping figure rose and showed her face. And it was a familiar face to each and every person in the room. Rising now, from Don Quixote's feet, was none other than the duchess' duenna, who had visited his room some nights before. And with her was her lovely fallen daughter, the girl who'd been seduced, whose lover had escaped her with her chastity. The duenna begged Quixote, once again to find the fugitive and bring him back to meet his obligations.

The duke and duchess stared in disbelief. (They had not planned this episode. Did this silly woman think that Don Quixote was a proper knight?)

"Good duenna, dry your tears," Quixote said. "I hereby swear to undertake your mission. I will find this villain, whom your daughter loves, and slay him if he will not keep his word."

The duke was quick to see a chance for entertainments. What fun! He would arrange a joust, between Quixote and the heartless suitor and see to it the rogue appeared. Not only that! The duke would offer weapons and a venue. The contest could take place within the castle yard.

What's this? The door flew open once again! This household fairly bustled with events. It was the page who'd visited

La Mancha. He'd come back with Teresa Panza's letters to her husband and the duchess.

The first note, for the duchess, read as follows:

Your High and Mightiness,

I am most happy to hear of my husband's being a governor and the news has cheered everyone in the village even though nobody believes it because everyone here thinks my husband is a blockhead and can't imagine his being good at governing anything other than a field of goats.

Thank-you for the lovely gifts.

Please, Your High and Mightiness ask my husband to send me some money so that I can go up to the capital and ride around in a fancy carriage and rub everyone's noses in my good fortune.

My daughter and son kiss your hands. Don't forget to write.

Teresa Panza.

The second letter was from Teresa Panza to her husband. The duchess read its contents to the group. (It is of course, despicable to read a letter not addressed to us. But this is not our fault. It's in the book.)

Dear Husband,

I got your letter and thought I would go mad with your good news. Our daughter, Sanchica, was so overjoyed she wet herself. Is this a dream? That a goatherd would get to be the governor of an island? Someday perhaps you'll get to be a tax collector and then you'll really get your hands on money!

Your lady the duchess will tell you that I intend to go to the capital and ride around in a carriage, which will make you look good.

The fountain in the village square's run dry and the pillory has been destroyed by lightning. I could not care less. Please let me know if you agree that I should ride about in a carriage in the capital for all to see. God keep you.

From your wife,
Teresa Panza.

We will not stop to contemplate the letters. Events are underway in Baratavia.

ᏅᎥᎥᎥᎤ

Sancho Panza lay in bed. Close to sleep, but sleepless, his thoughts were fixed on judgments and decisions. To be a great man – to be among the greatest of the hazelnuts upon this spinning seed we call our home, surely was exhausting. He tossed and turned, did Sancho. Poor hazelnut, he rolled about in bed. But then . . .

Dreadful sounds came crashing through the calm. (This really is a very noisy book.)

Bells and shouts. Sancho Panza threw aside his covers. Bugle blasts and drums. He listened hard and vaulted from the bed. In nothing but his nightshirt and his slippers, he opened up the doors into the hall.

Some twenty people thundered down the passageway, screaming, waving torches, swinging swords.

"To arms!" they cried. "Dear Governor! Our enemies are here! The island is invaded. Please arm yourself. You are our mighty leader."

"Arm myself?" cried Sancho. "What do I know of arms? This sort of thing is better left to knights. Perhaps you'd like to summon Don Quixote."

"We have brought your armor. You must put it on."

And they *had* brought him armor. At least they'd brought some armor of a sort. The crowd that gathered in the hall had brought two full-length wooden shields. They fastened him inside – one in front and one behind. They bound the shields around him with a rope. He was pinned, armored chin to toe. The army gave their governor a lance to hold. He leaned on it to keep from tipping over.

"March on!" they cried. "Inspire us to victory."

But Sancho Panza could not move an inch, so hampered was he by his makeshift armor.

"Carry me toward the fight," he said, "and prop me up or wedge me in a doorway."

No time. As the fight grew furious, he toppled. Trapped within the shields upon the floor, he lay there like a turtle in a shell. His little army, panicking, forgot him and Sancho soon was helpless, underfoot. Up and down the hallway surged his minions. Like the turtle he so much resembled, Sancho tried his best to pull his arms and feet and head inside his covering for shelter. "To arms!" his soldiers cried. "To arms! To arms!"

They tripped and stumbled over their great leader. They trampled him. They fell on him. One stood atop him for a time, not noticing on whom he stood, and shouted orders to the raging throng.

"Here boys!" he cried, "The enemy is pressing hard upon us. Shut the gate. Guard the entrance over there. Bring firepots and burning oil. Take mattresses and barricade the streets."

Inside his shell, Sancho Panza wept and prayed. *Oh, if only we would lose*, he thought, *so that this agony of war would cease.* (How many leaders, truth to tell, have had such secret wishes in their hearts?)

Finally, the enemy was vanquished. The palace hallway filled with shouts of joy. The crowd raised Sancho Panza to his feet.

Thus Sancho Panza's forces were victorious. But Sancho did not feel one bit a victor. He felt, instead, most keenly, a longing to no longer be a leader – a longing to regain his former life. He did not wish to be a mighty ruler, trampled like a turtle in the hall, a man who lives on candied fruit to keep his senses keen, whose cares infest his bed each night like fleas. Sancho asked his men for wine and bandages. He asked the time of day and hobbled to the stables all alone.

The sun was coming up, and here, lit by all the lovely honeyed pinks of dawn, was darling Dapple resting in his stall. Darling dusty Dapple, smelling sweet of hay and donkey coat; smelling, to the squire's nose, of love itself. Sancho threw his arms around the donkey's neck. Tenderly and crying tears, he held a quiet council with his beast.

"Come here, my dear companion, my good friend." Sancho kissed the donkey's velvet nose. "I was a happy man when my only duties centered on your care. I should have been content to occupy myself with the tasks of feeding you and tending to your tackle. Since I climbed the towers of ambition, my life has been a web of woes and worries."

He placed his saddle on his dearest friend. This would be his final act as ruler: to get up on his ass and ride away.

The members of his retinue were tricksters. Remember, they were servants of the duke. But when they learned their governor would leave them, they were truly sad to see him go.

The doctor tried to change his mind. He would allow the governor to eat whatever food he liked, however much.

"Too late," said Sancho Panza. "You're too late in cheeping, as the man said to the chicken who hatched out of the egg that he'd just eaten."

Sancho would not change his mind. "I know I was not born to be a governor," he said. "One should always keep in mind: don't stretch your legs out farther than your sheets will reach."

And with this pearl of philosophic insight, with embraces and with tears and vows of friendship, Sancho Panza's reign had reached its end.

Sancho had been governor ten days.

SANCHO PANZA DROPS INTO A HOLE; THE JOUST; THE ROAD TO SARAGOSSA.

⟨✦⟩

At the castle of the duke, arrangements for Quixote's joust were underway. Don Quixote was preparing to defend the duchess' duenna's sullied daughter. But there was a hitch he did not know of. The runaway young lover was in Flanders. The duke and duchess found this out and they had devised a secret plan. Without Quixote's knowing, the duke assigned a servant named Tosilos to take the lover's place and fight the joust. Tosilos would be covered in armor and no one, thought the duke, would be the wiser.

As the day approached, Quixote was joyous. Such contests were what knights like he were born for. He was happy – as is a colt let out to run, as is a singer who gets up on the stage to sing, as is any creature set loose to do whatever thing his soul most needs to do, and Don Quixote's soul was born to take on noble feats of derring-do.

As for Sancho Panza, reunited with his ass — his greatest friend who also was his means of transportation — he set out for the castle of the duke. He meant to reach the duke's estate by nightfall, but stopped awhile to socialize. By chance, he met with longtime friends. And so he had not reached the palace, when the sky began to dim above him.

With the darkness coming on, on a cloudy night without the light of stars, he decided he'd complete his trip when morning came. He left the road and rode into the forest in search of somewhere safe to spend the night.

In the gloom he came upon some small ramshackel buildings in the wood. Did Sancho Panza lift his eyes to make them out? Is this the reason Sancho Panza did not see the gaping hole that lay ahead directly in his path? Helplessly we watch as Sancho Panza and his ass fall into a yawning pit and out of sight.

They dropped down in the hole. He and Dapple dropped into the earth. Down and down they fell. Or so thought Sancho Panza. It seemed to him a very long way down. Sancho wondered if the chasm was, perhaps, the very pits of hell. The earth no longer underneath his donkey's hooves, Sancho Panza offered up his soul to God above. But God had no intention to receive him. Sancho landed only five yards down, still seated on the saddle on his donkey's back.

His drop abruptly over, Sancho felt around his chest, certain he was broken in a thousand parts. To his great surprise, he was unharmed. Dapple, on the other hand, had fallen into this hole not seated on a donkey, but sat on by a character famous all through literature for corpulence. Poor Dapple moaned in pain.

Sancho climbed down off his battered beast and felt about the cavern in the dark. The walls were smooth. There was no way to reach the rim above him.

"How strange a world," he thought out loud, "in which such things can happen. One day I am sitting on a throne and making judgments; the next day I am buried in the ground. We two old friends are sure to starve to death within this dark abyss. Why am I not Quixote? Why is this not the Cave of Montesinos? My master dropped into a place where every care and comfort was provided. He found before him emerald fields. He was welcomed in a shining crystal castle. But I will die here in the dark with Dapple. Someday, they will find our poor white bones. They will only know whose bones these were by virtue of our being found together, for they will know that Sancho Panza was a man who never would be parted from his donkey."

The night wore on. Dapple groaned. At last the sun began to rise, but by the pale gray dawn, Sancho saw no way to hoist himself up the cavern walls. Sancho joined his ass in wordless weeping.

The ass lay down. Sancho helped the aching animal to stand. He found a hunk of bread left in the saddlebags and, refusing to obey his own protesting stomach, he fed his friend.

Dapple chewed. Sancho looked around. He looked around and looked around again. And then. And then! How had he overlooked this? There was a portion of the wall – if he weren't mistaken, if his eyes did not play tricks, if this were not too splendid to be true – where there seemed to be a cranny in the wall. Sancho looked more closely. Was it possible that he had found a tunnel leading out? Taking up a stone, Sancho chipped the earth away. Before too long, he'd made the fissure large enough to let him through. Soon it would admit the ass as well.

Taking Dapple by the rope, Sancho led his injured donkey forward. He didn't know what lay ahead, of course. But Sancho Panza had no choice. There was dark ahead but doom behind. Man and beast, they groped their way along.

And then the dark subsided. Feeble threads of faintest light from high above.

୧୩୫୬

But back to Don Quixote and his contest.

The palace buzzed and hummed with preparations.

The servants took on details of the festival. There would be food and music. There would be decorations, installations, amusements, invitations: provisions for the many guests that go along with any great event.

In making ready for the fight, to sharpen the responses of his steed, Quixote took his horse out to the wood to run.

Did Rocinante run? We must resist the impulse to exaggerate, even if it makes the tale more thrilling. Probably he hurried right along. But not so fast he failed to spot a pothole that appeared right in their path along the trail.

Rocinante stopped.

The pothole was unusually deep. And it had further qualities which set this hole apart from others like it. This pothole had a voice, and lots to say.

"Hey, you up there," the pothole said. "Is anybody listening? Perhaps a knight who might take pity on a sinner, buried here while he is still alive?"

This was a pothole looking for a knight.

"Who's down there?" called Quixote. "Who cries out?"

"It is," the pothole cried again, "the governor of Baratavia, once squire to the great knight Don Quixote."

Oh, no. This was no ordinary pothole. This pothole claimed it was Quixote's squire! And then Quixote heard another voice he knew. Dapple! The ass sent up a string of hearty brays,

Overjoyed, we readers watch as Don Quixote rescues Sancho Panza. Men came from the duke's estate with ropes and cables, pickaxes and chains, to bring the squire and the ass to safety.

What were the chances of this happy ending? How lucky that Don Quixote and his rushing steed had stopped before the very hole that led into the earth above his squire. Thank heaven for the sort of chance that plots provide for worried readers of exciting tales.

❧

The morning of the joust arrived at last — the day on which our hero, Don Quixote, would teach the rascal-lover a thing or two about respecting promises. The banners flew, the trumpets blew, the common crowd was welcomed to the stands. For local folk, this was a special treat.

The two combatants suited up in armor and climbed upon their steeds, prepared to fight. Don Quixote and the scoundrel's stand-in rode into the castle yard. All eyes were on the knight and his opponent.

Tosilos, on his massive grizzled horse, made his way around the ring — a lap to show his mighty self before the crowd. But as he passed before the duchess' duenna and her daughter, he was conquered by a weapon not Quixote's.

Tosilos cast his eyes upon the girl, and he fell victim to a weapon much more devastating than a jouster's lance. Tosilos was the target of an arrow from the quiver of that age-old, knowing infant, that interfering baby we call Cupid.

The daughter! Tosilos had never seen a girl more beautiful. He knew at once the man whose place he'd taken for the contest was not only a rake, he was a fool. Tosilos raised his voice to stop the music. "I've changed my mind. I do not wish to fight. I will marry her at once. I declare that I am beaten, fair and square."

The roiling crowd fell silent. Pigeons settled to the ground and cooed. Tosilos took his helmet off to end the games.

But who was this – this man who had removed his visor to reveal his face? He was not the daughter's errant lover.

"This is a cheat!" the daughter cried. "They have put a servant in my husband's place."

A servant? In the errant lover's suit of armor? It made no sense to anyone who witnessed it.

But Don Quixote quickly saw the truth. "Enchanters make a habit of such ruses." So called the knight into the silent stands. Quixote had no doubt at all it was the errant lover on the other horse. He had been transformed to look just like Tosilos. Soon enough, he'd change back to his proper form. So the knight informed the puzzled crowd.

The duke, of course, was angry. His servant hadn't carried out his plan. All this fuss and bother and no joust.

But the duke knew better than to contradict his cherished dupe. Enchanters were to blame. Tosilos was escorted from the courtyard and then the Duke announced what would come next. The servant would be captive for two weeks, to give him time to become his proper self; the icy-hearted, lying, cheating ne'er-do-well, who was the apple of the daughter's eye.

Enchanters were to blame, the duke agreed.

But, by the time the duke had spelled this out, the daughter had a change of heart.

"Perhaps it is Tosilos, but I'll marry him."

Spoiled maidens mustn't be too picky. This damsel, she was reckless, but no fool.

⟮⟯

And so the great Quixote and his squire, their missions in the palace now put aside, were free to go. On the day that followed, the street filled up with well-wishers and curious, come to bid the famous pair goodbye. Altisidora, relentless and inventive (she was indeed a very gifted nuisance), did her best to poison the departure, accusing our two heroes of this and that. She tried, but failed to soil their good names.

And thus, the sojourn at the palace ended. The knight and squire left for Saragossa.

⟮⟯

Don Quixote and his squire came upon a meadow where a band of men had stopped to eat. The book reports the men were dressed as laborers (and it is likely laborers they were). Don Quixote rode up to the workmen, saluted them, and asked them for the purpose of their trip.

"We're taking precious sculptures to our town," said one.

"And would you be so kind as to let me see them?"

This worker was remarkably obliging. He left his lunch and took Quixote to inspect their cargo. The sculptures were the images of saints, whom Don Quixote recognized as knights.

There was St. George, on horseback, his sword thrust down the throat of an enormous snake.

"He was a great knight," said Don Quixote, "Not only that, but he defended maidens."

Here was St. Martin, on his horse as well, leaning down to offer half his coat to a poor stranger. "He was generous," said Quixote. "Perhaps he was more generous than brave."

Here was St. Paul, fallen on the road, struck down in his moment of conversion – the moment when he first believed in Jesus Christ.

And then St. James, high on his horse in battle, trampling on the heads of fallen foes – the Moors!

"These were men of God," said Don Quixote. "They conquered heaven by the force of arms. I am a sinner and fight in human ways, though up to now I don't know what I conquer."

The laborers wrapped up their precious relics, packed up their lunch, and went about their business.

⟨∞⟩

The next encounter caught our pair in fine green threads.

Don Quixote and his squire, passing through a lovely leafy forest, found themselves entangled in a web.

Whose ruse was this? Quixote knew. It was enchanters, to be sure. Don Quixote cursed and flailed and fought, the web becoming tighter with each spin. Don Quixote's captors, it turned out, were not enchanters this time, but enchantresses: two lovely maidens dressed as shepherdesses. They were as pretty as the dawn, wearing golden skirts and bedecked in laurel garlands – their hair as golden as the sun.

"Stop, Sir Knight!" one lovely creature cried. "Those nets are not to do you harm, but merely for our pastime. If you will hold still, we will release you."

And as the knight and squire were untangled, other figures came forth from the trees. The knight and squire had come upon a group of revelers, some thirty souls or more, who passed the day by dressing up as rural folk, pretending they were people of Arcadia (a long-ago, imaginary place).

They dressed as shepherds and their mates, in finery. They'd learned a dash of poetry to speak (as shepherds did in literary works). They'd pitched their pretty tents next to the river. They'd strung the trees with nets to catch the passing birds to make a feast. And who, they asked, had fallen into their trap?

It was Don Quixote and his squire? Why, these were very famous folk they'd caught. The people of Arcadia recognized our heroes' names at once. It seems the story of the knight had made its way to every inch of Spain.

"This gentleman," cried one of the shepherdesses, "is none other than the bravest and most lovesick knight who ever lived!"

Above their heads, the nets filled up with colored birds, driven from the branches by the happy hubbub down below.

Of course, Quixote and his squire were offered every sort of hospitality, and welcomed at a feast among the trees. And once the colored birds were down their gullets, once the wine was drunk and songs were sung, Don Quixote rose to offer thanks.

"They say the worst of sins is pride, but I insist the worst sin is ingratitude. And to show my gratitude, I will stand for two days on the road. I will stop each traveler I meet and demand that they affirm out loud that these two lovely maidens who caught me in their net are the loveliest of any who exist in any time or place with the one exception of my Lady Fair."

Whatever were the benefits of such an offer to his hosts – even to the maidens who were singled out – Quixote's gesture was accepted gladly.

The shepherds and the shepherdesses followed Don Quixote and his squire, who took up posts, standing in the middle of the road.

"You passengers and travelers," the knight called out. "Knights and squires and all on foot or horseback. Know that Don Quixote will have you swear that other than his mistress Dulcinea, no maidens are more beautiful or courteous than the nymphs who play here in these woods!"

Now, travelers did come along the road. But they were not on horseback, nor on foot. And they were not the sort who could ever be convinced to slow their pace to judge a maiden's beauty.

There was a distant roar. The road began to shake, the trees to tremble. Whatever thing this was, was coming closer.

It was not knights or squires, but running bulls.

"Stop! You scurvy knaves!" Quixote shouted. "Confess," he cried, "that all the things I have proclaimed are true!"

The bulls, if they had heard him, did not heed him. They thundered past. They trampled him and Sancho in the dust.

"Stay!" Quixote shouted in their wake.

They did not stop. The cowards! They did not even stop to look behind them. They disappeared, vast and disobedient, leaving in their wake our broken heroes.

Indignity. The bulls had paid Quixote no attention. People of that time and place had a winsome phrase that puts it nicely: They gave him no more thought than last year's clouds.

A Change of Plans; The Battle of
the Breeches; A Famous Bandit.

The next day, Don Quixote and his squire found lodging at an inn. And to Sancho Panza's great relief, the knight knew that the inn was not a castle. The dusty pair was shown up to their rooms.

Castles, as you know, have walls of stone – walls that keep a castle cool and quiet. Inns have walls of wood instead, some as thin as paper. Encounters in such places can be overheard. Voices drift between the rooms.

Don Quixote and his squire did not mean to overhear the travelers within the room next door. In fact, they were quite helpless to prevent it. But it was fortunate they did so. It turns out the talk they heard was on a subject very close to home.

"I beg you, Don Geronimo," a voice crept through the walls. "While we wait for dinner to be brought, let's read another chapter of the second part of Don Quixote of La Mancha."

"Don Juan, I'd rather not," another voice could clearly be discerned. "This book I hold is nonsense. No one who has read Part I could possibly take pleasure from the second."

"All the same," the first went on, "there is no book so bad that there's nothing good in it. Although I must admit it's disagreeable that in this second part, Don Quixote does not love his lady."

Don Quixote stood. He strained his ears. And then he spoke out in a booming voice, meant to pierce the walls and reach the strangers. "If anybody dares state that Don Quixote of La Mancha no longer loves the Lady Dulcinea, I will force him to acknowledge he is wrong. The peerless Dulcinea could never be forgotten. Quixote is not capable of doing so."

Silence from the other room, and then a voice responding: "Who is that?"

Sancho Panza answered. "It is Don Quixote of La Mancha."

Another silence, then the sound of footfall.

Two gentlemen came through Quixote's door, every bit as puzzled as our heroes. Instantly, they recognized they'd come upon the very man – the knight – the character they'd read about in Part I of the famous book.

"You are he! There is no doubt," said one. He fell on Don Quixote and embraced him. "You are Don Quixote. It seems that someone has usurped your name and has tried to cloud your brilliance with a pack of lies."

There was a book, they told the knight. A second book describing his adventures. One of the strangers held it out. This second book was not by Benengeli.

Don Quixote took the book. He turned its pages quietly. He frowned and closed its covers. The knight would not debase himself by reading it.

"What does it say of me?" asked Sancho Panza.

"It says you are a simpleton." It was Don Geronimo (the second voice), who spoke. "It says that you are not at all amusing. It says you are a glutton and a souse. It says that you are not at all the character the world became so fond of in Part I."

The landlord came with dinner.

Sancho and the landlord ate in Sancho's room. The landlord and the squire ate and drank. And drank. And drank and drank. The innkeeper, so says the book, was "tangle-footed" by the evening's end. Tangle-footed, as no doubt was Sancho.

The two fine gentlemen took Quixote to their room to eat, and told him of the contents of the false Part II. One instance: in the second book, Don Quixote goes to Saragossa.

This, of course, had been Quixote's plan.

And so, a change of plans, right then and there. Quixote would not go to Saragossa. He would outwit the blackguard with the lying quill. And so to bed.

Tomorrow it would be an early start. On to Barcelona.

⁕

They traveled for six days, making sure they took a route that brought them nowhere close to Saragossa.

These days passed without incident, the story goes, but on the sixth day, the plot resumes anew.

⁕

Our heroes were extremely worn from journeying and found a copse of oak trees in which they could take shelter for the night.

Sancho Panza, simple sort, fell right to sleep. But Don Quixote lay awake, bitten by his many fleas of worry. And chief among the buzzing pests was this: the Lady Dulcinea still had not been rescued from her spell. She was abroad upon the spinning world – somewhere out there in the Spanish night – a peasant girl, and not the sort that's pleasant to cast eyes on; not the sort one likes to be downwind of.

But what could Don Quixote do to save her? Her fate did not lie in his hands, but in the pudgy clutches of the squire. Sancho had agreed, we know, to lash himself to break the spell. But there he lay asleep. The ignoramus! His backside was entirely unscathed.

Don Quixote scratched and rolled and pondered this dilemma in the dark.

Sancho snored and drooled, peaceful and infuriating on the ground. This peasant would be Dulcinea's savior?

And then Quixote had an inspiration.

Merlin had insisted that Sancho must administer the beating on his own. But was this so? It's possible that Merlin was mistaken. Increasingly, it seemed to Don Quixote, watching Sancho Panza slumber on, that Sancho might indeed be beaten by another hand. Why not? What harm could come from trying? Whatever Merlin had decreed, thought Don Quixote, the point was that the backside must be beaten. By whom? It couldn't really matter very much.

Don Quixote rose. He took the reins from Rocinante's neck and made a whip. He crept to where his squire lay asleep, stooped, and placed his hands on Sancho's breeches.

The squire woke up quickly (as one would).

"What's this? Who is unlacing me?" cried Sancho.

"I unlace you!" said Quixote angrily, as if this awkward moment were the squire's fault. "Dulcinea languishes while you do nothing. I will pay the debt you owe by lashing you myself."

"You will not," said Sancho. He was, by now, entirely alert. "The lashes I receive I must deliver, and right now I am not inclined to do so."

And so (would I could spare you this), a wrestling match ensued between our heroes. The prize would be control of Sancho's breeches. Thank heaven that they struggled in the dark. It's not the sort of imagery that one day will be chiseled into sculpture and carried with great care from town to town.

To hurry forward, then, to a conclusion: Sancho won the battle by brute strength. He pinned Quixote on the ground and made his master swear a solemn oath. Never would he launch a new assault upon the other's pants. Sancho Panza let his master up and wandered off to find a spot to sleep.

Sancho moved away into the oaks, but he did not lie down at once. He leaned against a tree. He'd had, of course, the rudest of awakenings. He needed time to gather up his thoughts.

It was almost morning, but still dark. The trees above him rustled and something brushed against the squire's head. Sancho lifted up his face. He stretched a groping hand into the leaves. What was this? The branches up above him bore strange fruit. Oh, no! They bore not fruit, but boots! Strange boots and legs as well.

Horrified, he hollered out Quixote's name. In that one moment Quixote was forgiven and soon the knight was at his squire's side. Above our heroes, in the trees, hung the bodies of some thirty men.

"Bandits," said Quixote. "They are outlaws. In this part of Spain they're hanged from trees."

Dead bandits, hanging by the dozens in the trees. What could be more unnerving for the knight and squire? Very soon they were to have an answer.

Forty bandits, not the least bit passed away, surrounded our good heroes in the wood. And here was Don Quixote undefended; his lance leaned up against a tree. Furthermore, the knight was not upon his horse. Rocinante dozed nearby, unbridled. To be so caught off guard was most unknightly. Don Quixote bowed his head and crossed his hands. Here was more indignity to bear. The outlaws swarmed upon the knight and squire and took whatever they could find in Sancho's bags.

Then suddenly, the crime was interrupted. Another figure on a mighty horse.

This newcomer was large and hale and hearty, dark and stern – a man of maybe thirty-four or five. He wore a coat of chain mail and called out that the ransacking must stop. He turned to Don Quixote and saw the sadness in Quixote's face.

"Do not be sorrowful," he said. "You have not fallen into the hands of some unworthy cutthroat rogue. I am Roque Guinart, whose ways are more of kindness than of cruelty."

It was a very well-known name. Don Quixote knew it right away: the legendary Roque Guinart – the bandit king.

"My sorrow," said Quixote, "does not derive from being at your mercy. I am Don Quixote of La Mancha, whose deeds are known around the world, and yet I find that I am apprehended without my lance in hand. Here I stand, unhorsed and quite defenseless. Great knights are never caught so unaware."

Guinart knew of Don Quixote. (The people in these woods, it seems, read lots of books.) Yet it had not occurred to him that the knight he'd read about was flesh and blood – a man and not a storyteller's fancy. And now the two celebrities were face-to-face.

"Oh, valiant knight," said Roque Guinart. "You must not be disheartened by what might seem, at first, to be bad luck. Sometimes such things can turn your fortunes to the better."

Roque Guinart then made a friendly gesture. He ordered that his men return what they had stolen from the squire's bags.

With that he turned to other bandit business.

He bade his bandits fall in line and shared among the company the spoils of a recent heist.

"If one were not so fair," said Roque Guinart, "it would not be possible to lead these men."

Now Sancho Panza, recently a ruler, knew something of the business of commanding men. He understood the conduct of great hazelnuts. He puffed his chest and spoke his thoughts aloud.

"Justice is so fine a thing," said Sancho, "it's even proper conduct in dealing with such thieves as these."

Oh, could the squire never leave a thought unsaid? Could he not, for once, be circumspect?

One among the bandits took offence. (Though thief he was, he did not like the word.) Indeed, he was about to bring his musket down on Sancho's head, when new events came bursting through the bushes. More bandits, scouts on horseback with this news: a little band of travelers approached.

"Are these the sort of travelers we look for?" asked Guinart. "Or are they the sort of travelers who look for us?"

"They are the sort we look for," said a scout.

Said the leader, "Capture them and bring them here at once."

When the travelers arrived, it turned out they were just the sort of travelers that bandits hope for in their dearest dreams. Two gentlemen on horses, both with footmen; two pilgrims – men of God who went on foot – and finally, a coach containing ladies, a trail of servants following behind. They were unarmed and carried with them money and possessions for their journeys.

Roque Guinart asked them for their names and destinations.

A gentleman on horseback spoke up first: "We're captains in the Spanish infantry," he said. "We're bound for Barcelona to board a ship to take us off to Sicily, in service of the crown."

The pilgrims answered next. They were men of God, embarking on a pilgrimage to Rome.

And then the ladies in the coach. A maiden spoke up bravely from the window. "This is the coach of Dona Guiomar de Quinones." She gestured at her mistress. "With her are her daughter and her maid and a duenna. They will board a ship that's bound for Naples."

What luck. There would be fat pickings from this little group, who began to plead and beg for mercy. They knew the legend of this famous bandit.

Now when it comes to bandits, begging isn't worth your while. Theft is their profession, after all. But Roque Guinart was famous for two reasons. First of all he was a wily bandit. But also he was known for showing mercy.

On this day, he lived up to his legend. He told his men that they should not take every thing the pleading, weeping travelers possessed. His victims dried their eyes and gave their thanks.

And now the bandit turned to Don Quixote.

"This way of life might well seem strange to you," he said. "The truth is this: long ago I was the victim of a great injustice. I never found a way to take revenge. I am by nature good and well-intentioned and yet, my need to set things straight still burns. It overrides my law-abiding nature. One sin that I commit calls forth another. And on and on I go in life, into the maze that is my own confusion."

And so he made his living robbing travelers, but kind deep down and good at heart, he let them keep a little now and then.

"Better suited for a friar than a bandit."

It was a whispered voice, a voice from somewhere in among the men. "He's generous, not only with his own money, but with the treasure that his men have earned."

Whoever owned the whispered voice had bargained that his leader would not hear him. But sharp-eared, sharp-eyed Roque Guinart heard each word, and looking all about him, found its source.

Roque Guinart raised his sword. The whisperer would not complain again. His poor complaining head was cut in two.

The thievery complete, the rebel killed, the great Guinart remembered Don Quixote. Guinart took out his writing instruments. He wrote a note that Don Quixote did not read.

It was a letter to a friend in Barcelona, to let him know that Don Quixote and his squire – famous and hilarious, the subjects of the celebrated book – were on their way to visit Barcelona. Guinart would bring the silly knight himself.

He sent the letter on ahead, by bandit.

Our Heroes Arrive
in Barcelona; The Talking Bust;
The Printing Shop

∽⟡∽

On the very morning Roque Guinart had predicted in the letter he had written to his friend, Don Quixote and Sancho Panza found themselves delivered to the Barcelona beach.

Before them was the sea, the blue and shining sea. Endless, sparkling in the sun. It was nothing like the lakes around La Mancha – like nothing Don Quixote and his squire had ever seen. A dazzling sort of boundlessness to swell the heart. Here they were again, the knight and squire, balanced on the rim of new adventures.

On the sea were galleys, great ships that dropped their awnings as the sun arose. They wouldn't need their awnings to keep off the rain. Not today. The sun was out and shining bright. The ships were decked with streamers. Banners fluttered on the masts. Light and color, beach and sky and sand.

It was St. John the Baptist's Day – a day of festival, of Christian celebration, a day to welcome summer to this Spanish shore.

Bugles played, and trumpets. Cannons boomed and echoed. On the city walls and on the forts, guns went off in answer to the cannons. It was a kind of carnival for eyes and ears. And then the smell of seaside. Can anything in all the lovely world lift the heart like sun and crashing waves?

Four men with smiling faces galloped forth on horseback, calling out their greetings, calling to be heard above the waves and guns.

"Welcome! Welcome to our city, oh great pinnacle of all knight-errantry. Oh, knight to shine above all other knights. Welcome, great Quixote – the genuine Quixote, described for all to know by Benengeli, flower of the greatest of historians."

It was Roque Guinart's friend, Don Antonio Moreno, who'd come to meet our heroes to ask them to accept his hospitality. Would they accept? They would accept with pleasure, having slept so many, many nights upon the ground.

But the devil never sleeps. Benengeli says it time and time again. And on this day, the devil made his presence known by means of little boys who followed the procession from the beach. They scurried up behind Quixote's horse and Sancho's ass and found a way to lift the creatures' tails and lodged sharp brambles in places that normally are properly and modestly concealed beneath the tail.

Such agony! And every time the horse and donkey dropped their tails the pain grew worse. The beasts reared up and Don Quixote and his squire found themselves upon the ground amid a laughing crowd.

And so began their stay in Barcelona.

Now, Moreno was wealthy and intelligent, and had the kind of extra time that wealthy people in this tale enjoy. Once inside his sprawling house, further fun and games were underway. He bid Quixote take the heavy armor off. (He'd traveled far. He must be very weary.) And then Moreno bid his guests come out on the balcony to greet the crowds.

There was Don Quixote, dressed only in his underclothes. Quixote waved. Sancho beamed and nodded. They didn't know this was a city feast day; they guessed the carnival below was all for them. Outside on the streets, the throng looked up and waved and cheered, not knowing who these lunatics might be.

⌒⟋⟍⌒

Guests arrived and lunch was served and stories gaily traded back and forth. Don Quixote told of his adventures. Sancho Panza was his most amusing self – the comic boisterous presence of the books.

And when the lunch was over, there were more surprises for the knight. With whispers and on tiptoes, Don Moreno took Quixote down the hall and through the doorway of a distant room.

"I am uncomfortable with secrets, and so I am relieved to have you here. Now you must swear," he said to Don Quixote, "you will tell no one what you are about to see. The door is closed. The lock is locked. Promise me you'll never tell a soul about the miracle that I'm about to show you."

"I swear," said Don Quixote. "I have ears to hear but, be assured, I have no tongue to speak. Whatever lies within your breast can find a home in mine. Please know that it will never be divulged."

On a pedestal there was a bust – a sculpture of a head made out of stone. Such treasures were not unusual in houses such as this, but this bust, said the Duke, was very special.

"This head was made by powerful enchanters," said the host. "It can answer any question. Now, we won't ask it anything today. It will not answer questions on a Friday. As today is Friday, we will wait. You have one day to come up with your questions."

༺☙༻

Sancho spent the afternoon enjoying all the pleasures of the household. He ate and drank and prattled on and made himself the subject of attention. Quixote, on the other hand, was taken on a tour of town, upon a great imposing horse, and dressed up in a brand-new, handsome coat.

The coat was a fine gift from Don Moreno, but Don Moreno's generosity had strings attached. On the sly he'd had a sign affixed to Don Quixote's back. "This is Don Quixote of La Mancha" read the sign.

Passersby who read the sign called out to Don Quixote – called his name.

"This is a great advantage of knighthood," said Quixote. "I am famous to the edges of the earth."

Plainly put, Quixote was a laughingstock. Though mercifully, it seems, he never knew this.

There was to be no end to Don Moreno's pranks. What would a day of celebration be without a ball? And Don Moreno's wife, who shared her husband's flair for stuff and nonsense, made sure the fun would last into the night. There was a splendid dinner and when the dinner ended – very late – the lady had arranged that there be dancing. She'd chosen two close friends (modest, so the story says, but lively), whose task it was to seem to be enamored.

They took Quixote to the floor for every dance. They spun the knight about the room. They giggled and they squeaked at him and flattered him. They frolicked and they tugged at him and turned him to and fro. They billed and cooed and chucked him underneath his sagging chin. Long into the night and early morning, they showed a sort of vim and bounce and gusto that would have left the heartiest among us longing for the comforts of the crypt.

They bore down on the knight with their flirtation, with charm so unrelenting that finally, Quixote, truly almost weeping with exhaustion, collapsed into a heap upon the ballroom floor.

He begged, "Ladies, you must manage your desires. I am promised to the Lady Dulcinea. She is the only lady of my thoughts."

The knight could dance no more, could not even stand upon his own two feet. With Sancho in attendance, Don Moreno had Quixote gathered up and carried off. The plaything was retired for the night.

Upstairs in Don Quixote's room, Sancho tucked his master into bed. Carefully he pulled Quixote's covers up to keep him warm. He knew his master must not risk a chill.

⟨⟨⟨⟩⟩⟩

A word with you before we leave this scene.

Quixote's always quick to call his squire names: a nincompoop, a moron, or a lout. He does not listen to his squire's worries. And we can argue, from this time to kingdom come, whether Don Quixote loved his squire; whether Don Quixote ever loved another soul upon our little spinning mustard seed. Not to be unfair to Don Quixote. There are people who have wondrous things to offer up to others, but sometimes selfless love is not among them. Perhaps our Sancho knew this in his heart. But Sancho (booby, lout, and nincompoop) did not need his master's love to love him, so wise and good was Don Quixote's squire.

But we must slip from Don Quixote's bedroom. He's earned his rest and we must not delay it.

Good night, good knight, little lamb within a den of wolves.

⌇

The next day was not Friday. The bust, remember, did not work on Fridays. The time arrived for Don Moreno and his guests to ask their questions of the magic head. The few who were invited to the session were: Don Quixote, Sancho Panza, two friends of Don Moreno, and the modest, lively ladies who, the night before, had worn out Don Quixote on the dance floor.

Don Moreno was the first to ask his questions.

"Tell me bust, what are my thoughts?"

All stared in silence at the magic head.

A voice as clear as daylight seemed to rise up from the very air. "I do not divine thoughts."

Who spoke? A gust of fear blew through the room like wind.

One of the dancing ladies now addressed the head. "Tell me what must I do to become beautiful?"

A moment while the marble head considered. "Be virtuous," the voice replied. "Be chaste."

Now her friend approached the bust and cleared her throat. "Tell me, statue. Does my husband love me?"

"Consider how he treats you," said the bust, "and you will have the answer that you seek."

This was common sense, of course, but true.

A gentleman stood forward. "Tell me, head, what are the wishes of my son and heir?"

"Why, he would like to bury you," the bust replied.

"I know this to be true," the man agreed.

One by one, the guests stepped forth with questions, Quixote and his squire were last in line.

"Tell me," asked Quixote, "oh you, who answers wisely and so well, were the events that I reported in the Cave of Montesinos real events? Will Sancho Panza go about his lashings? Will Lady Dulcinea be restored?"

"About the Cave of Montesinos," said the bust, "there is a little bit of truth, a little fantasy. Sancho Panza's lashings will take time. The Lady Dulcinea will regain her perfect form."

His questions answered, Don Quixote moved aside.

Sancho Panza asked the statue this: "Will I be a governor again? Will I always be a lowly squire? Will I ever see my wife and children?"

"You will govern in your house, if you return there," came the voice. "If you go home, you'll see your wife and children. When you cease to serve a knight, you will cease, as well, to be a squire."

***

Mr. Benengeli, interrupts the story for a secret. The magic bust was not the least bit magic. Some time ago, Don Moreno had seen a bust like this while visiting the city of Madrid. Returning to his home, he'd had one made. Beneath the hollow head there ran a tube which led down to a room below the floor. Don Moreno's nephew, waiting there, heard the questions and provided answers.

***

One afternoon, Don Quixote and his squire, escorted by two servants from the villa, took a stroll through town to see the sights. They came upon a shop that bore a sign: "Books Printed Here." As Don Quixote'd never seen a printing shop, and as he was a literary hero, he was very keen to go inside.

It was a busy business. Inside the shop, men were printing in one place, correcting in another, setting type (putting all the letters in the proper place), doing all the many things that are involved in turning out a book.

The workers in the printing shop were friendly, and willing to put work aside to show the knight the books they had underway that afternoon.

There was a little book, *La Bagatelle*, sayings and reflections in Italian. How charming other languages can be! Ideas that are obvious are made to seem enticingly opaque! Another book, *Light of The Soul*, had to do with solemn Godly matters – a book that sinners might do well to buy. Quixote said this as he looked it over. How useful was an author who could help the reading public mend its ways!

But then there was among these books, books with very much to recommend them, a book that caught Quixote's gaze and held it. It was *The Second Part of the Ingenious Hidalgo Don Quixote of La Mancha*. It was the book that falsely claimed to be the further stories of Quixote's life.

"I've heard of this." A blush arose on Don Quixote's cheeks. "Although I am surprised it's not been burned, owing to its insolence. This is lies. Histories are only good and pleasurable to read if they approach the truth."

Fuming, Don Quixote, left the shop.

In the days that followed, Don Moreno did his best to wring amusements from his unsuspecting visitor. They spent a day aboard the galleys moored offshore: were witness to a battle and a capture. But these are stories that, though entertaining, we will leave aside. We will move on to a moment which would change Quixote's life for good and all.

The Knight of The White Moon;
Sancho Panza solves a Problem;
Tosilos; Six Hundred Pigs.

⊙⟪⟫⊙

It was morning. Don Quixote took a ride with Sancho on the beach. He was wearing all his armor. As you know, a knight must be prepared. And what a lucky thing this was, because approaching on the beach there was another knight, also in his armor, with a shining moon upon his shield.

Once he was in earshot, the stranger called across the wind and sand:

"Oh, Don Quixote. Fearless Don Quixote of La Mancha. Illustrious and noble Don Quixote. I am the famous Knight of The White Moon. I'm sure you will have heard of me, owing to my exploits. I have come to challenge you, to test your mighty arm, to force you to acknowledge that my Lady Fair, whoever she may be, is more beautiful by far than Dulcinea. If you confess this to me now and do not fight, I will spare you. But if you choose to fight me and I defeat you, I will demand you put aside your calling as a knight for one full year. I will order that you go back to your village and put away your sword. If you are the victor, my life will likewise be at your disposal."

Quixote was bewildered by this challenge, by the arrogance and gall of his opponent, and by the strange conditions he demanded.

"Knight of The White Moon, of whom I've never heard before this very moment, if you had laid eyes on my Lady Dulcinea, you would never be so foolish as to ask for the confession that you do. There has not now, nor has there ever been, loveliness that is comparable to hers. I accept your challenge on the spot. Choose your ground and I will do the same."

Soon a crowd had gathered on the beach. It was the city's great and small, sensing confrontation in the air. Among the watching crowd was Don Moreno. But this was not a game that he'd devised.

There were no blasts from trumpets. There was no sound of bells, no bugles, and no banners to announce the coming battle on the sand. The knights rode off to make a proper distance. They turned and, to the call of gulls and crash of waves, began the charge.

We will not lay blame. We won't point out, for instance, Rocinante's defects as a mount – his age and his fragility and timid soul. Old friend, he'd served his master well for many years. So we will turn our eyes instead to look upon the beast who bore the other knight. He was strong and fast and sturdy and a creature well configured for a joust. He plunged and pawed and thundered forth and in the blinking of an eye he'd made his way a full two-thirds across the course that lay between the knights.

The Knight of The White Moon raised up his lance. On his charging steed, he bore down on our weak and withered hero, but raised the tip too high to hit Quixote squarely in the chest. It seems he had no wish to take Quixote's life. But he would knock him off his mount and did. Don Quixote tumbled off his horse into the sand.

The Knight of The White Moon jumped from off his mighty beast and pinned Quixote's visor with his lance.

"You are a dead man," said the victor to Quixote, "unless you say 'My Lady Fair – whoever she may be – is lovelier by far than Dulcinea.'"

"Then kill me," said Quixote. "Dulcinea del Toboso is the loveliest of any maiden born. My weakness should not obscure that truth. Kill me. Take away my life. You have already rid me of my honor."

"No," the other knight replied. "I will not take your life. And long live the Lady Dulcinea. Go home. And stay there for one year. I ask no more."

The Knight of The White Moon bowed his head, turned his horse away, and cantered off.

Don Quixote lay upon the ground, a crumpled, conquered character, a wounded bird. Those in the crowd who knew him lifted up his visor to reveal his face, pale and bathed in sweat and full of sorrow. Sancho Panza couldn't think what he must do or say. Here was his friend and master, who would not be a knight for one full year. And Sancho would no longer be a squire. (He worried for himself, as well, of course.) The broken knight was picked up off the sand and taken to the city in a chair.

And so in those few moments, Don Quixote's knighthood was repealed. Sometimes great events in life are unannounced – they creep up, unexpected. They come upon you quietly and tap you on the shoulder.

⁊⁊⁊

Reader, do you wonder who this other knight might be, the white moon shining on his shield; this knight who had defeated Don Quixote? Benengeli lets us know the truth. The knight who has just conquered Don Quixote was none other than the Bachelor Carrasco. Did you guess? Don Quixote and his squire did not know and never would. They are not readers of this book, but characters.

⁊⁊⁊

Don Quixote was taken to Moreno's house. Quixote did not leave his bed for days. Defeated and morose, he lay, his bony face turned to the wall. He stared and sighed. His eyes were plums. Sancho Panza did not leave his side.

"One year," Quixote said to Sancho Panza, although he spoke this facing to the wall. "One year and I'll return to my profession. And when I do you will become an earl."

⁐

Don Quixote did not put on his armor for the journey home. He could not wear the costume of a knight. He was, he said, no longer so entitled.

Sancho Panza bundled up the armor and fastened it to Dapple's back.

The two left Barcelona with no fanfare, stopping only briefly to look back.

"Barcelona!" said the knight, gazing on the city in the distance. "Behind us is the place where my bad luck and cowardice robbed me of my glory as a knight. There I felt the changing whims of fortune. The luster of my reputation was made dim. My happiness came crashing down around me."

For five days they made their way toward La Mancha. Benengeli writes that of this passage there is not much to tell. Just weariness. Just sadness on the journey.

However, there's one incident the Moor records. I'll stop to tell this story, for though it's not important in the larger scheme, it might serve to distract us from our sorrows.

Our heroes came upon a group of men in argument.

As Don Quixote and his squire approached, one among the crowd called out, pointing out our heroes to his friends. "Hello! One of these travelers will help us with our problem. They do not know the parties to each side."

Here is the problem that the group described:

A villager, so fat he weighed three hundred pounds, had asked another villager to race him. The second villager weighed just one hundred pounds. They would run a race on foot.

The fat man had requested that his small opponent run his race carrying two hundred pounds in weights. This, he'd said, would even up their chances, and this would make the running contest fair. But was this fair? The members of the crowd could not agree.

They looked to Don Quixote for an answer. (He seemed to be the leader of the two.) But Don Quixote didn't have an answer. No, this was not the knight we used to know. There was a time, you will recall, when Quixote was an expert in so many fields: astronomy, geography, ethics, navigation, comportment, spells, aerodynamics.

Don Quixote stepped aside. "I'm so confused," he said. "I am not even fit to feed a cat."

And so the puzzle fell to Sancho Panza. It was a stroke of luck for all involved. Sancho – former foremost hazelnut – had recently discovered (as you know) that he had quite a knack for solving problems. He gave the race some thought, and found the very heart of the conundrum.

"There is a tradition to such matters," said our Sancho. "The man who is challenged to the fight is properly the one who sets the rules. Otherwise the challenger (the fat man) will set such rules that mean that his opponent cannot win. And so the thinner man must set the rules. If the fat man insists that the weight of the two runners should be equal, he must be the one to make it so. He must somehow make himself much smaller. The two men then will weigh the same and they will run the race on equal terms."

Yes indeed! Here was a solution. The fat man must somehow reduce his bulk. "He must lop off a full two hundred pounds," said Sancho, "from any portion of his body that he pleases."

"He will not wish to do so," said a member of the crowd.

"That's true," chimed in another, "and the skinny man will not agree to run with weights. Perhaps the best solution is that all the money we had kept for wagers be spent, instead, on drinking at the tavern."

And so it was decided.

Clever Sancho Panza. Clever squire. The crowd was grateful for his time and wisdom. They murmured admiration in the squire's wake as he and Don Quixote took the road.

"If the servant is so clever," said the crowd, "how very brilliant must the master be?"

That night our heroes slept beneath the stars.

⌒⫘⌒

On the road the next day, our two travelers encountered a fellow that we know.

Tosilos. He was the servant of the duke who had pretended, for the purpose of a duel, that he was the rascal lover of the duchess' duenna's ruined daughter.

Tosilos had called off the fight. Do you recall? Once he'd cast his eyes upon the girl, he'd said he'd marry her.

Well, things had turned out badly for Tosilos. The duke would not be thwarted in his pleasures, and those who disobeyed him would regret it.

Tosilos had been lashed a hundred times. And furthermore, no marriage would take place between Tosilos and the girl. This girl, she would be no one's wife. The duke had sent her off to join a nunnery.

And so a happy ending was averted.

But was this man who said he was Tosilos really he? Don Quixote told his squire he did not think so. He reminded Sancho Panza that enchanters could make any man appear to be Tosilos if they wished.

Homeward. Quixote and his squire retraced their steps, plodding sadly back toward La Mancha. They came upon the place where they had dined with shepherds and with shepherdesses, pretty as the dawn. Such a happy time that was; friendship in the dappled wood, a feast of colored birds, a toast.

Don Quixote stopped to reminisce. He called up merry memories, and as he did, his weary soul began to stir, like a watered plant will lift its leaves. And then, there in the cheeping chirping sunlit forest, something of a plan began to form.

Perhaps Quixote could not be a knight. Perhaps his squire could not be a squire. Perhaps for one full year they could not be the characters who live in books of chivalry.

But they could take example from another bookish fashion of the time. They could take up (could they not?) the perfect, peaceful world of former simpler days. Arcadia! Perhaps, Quixote thought, they could be shepherds.

"Shepherds!" Don Quixote said to Sancho. "I shall buy some sheep." Inspiration followed inspiration. "I will be the shepherd named Quixotiz. You can be Panzino. I think that name will suit you very well. The Bachelor Carrasco – he could be a shepherd named Sansonino. Our friend the barber could be called Miculoso. The priest?

Perhaps he'd be the shepherd Curiambro. Surely they will all want to join in."

Sancho saw the promise in the scheme. "And I could call my wife Teresona. That name would suit her fatness, and is so like her present name Teresa. And Sanchica," said the squire, "she could bring us dinner in the fields."

"We'll wander here and there throughout the mountains," said Quixote. "We'll sing and we'll lament and we will drink the dancing water of the springs. What will we eat? The bounty of the oak trees! And when we tire, we'll rest beneath the willows and breathe into our lungs the roses' scents. The flowers on the meadows will be the carpets underneath our feet. And from all this beauty, and because the gods will bless us with their many gifts, we will be inspired to lovely thoughts. We will write great poems, by means of which we will become renowned, not only in our present time, but for as long as humankind exists." (As people who aren't authors are aware, writing is much simpler than it looks.)

The future thus so cheerfully decided, Sancho Panza slept his deepest sleep that night.

But somewhere in Quixote's soul, a doubt had not been quelled. His thoughts rose up and buzzed about his head.

Have you ever tried to sleep and yet could not? And in this state have you ever lain awake next to someone who is sleeping? Why should they – one asks oneself – have the bliss of sleep while you do not? It is a special kind of misery, this wakefulness as next to you another drools and dreams. (Have they no cares? Are they so deeply dull of mind that nothing can disrupt their stupid slumber?)

Luckily the problem can be solved. (I'll tell you this. Someday you'll find it useful.) You will find your spirit soothed if you can find a way to wake the simpleton who dozes at your side.

This Quixote did. He woke the squire. And once he had his servant's full attention, he filled the air with grudges and rebukes. Chief among his grievances was this: would Sancho Panza ever get around to punishing his fat and spoiled backside? The Lady Fair was still not disenchanted. When would Sancho take this task in hand? As far as Don Quixote was concerned this night would be as good a time as any. Why should the squire wait another moment?

"Sir," said Sancho Panza (pointing out the obvious, I think), "I'm not some monk — not the sort to get up in the middle of the night to take a whip to my own blameless flesh."

"You stony-hearted creature," said the knight. "Think of all the many things I've done for you."

Thus, stony-hearted Sancho was faced with what might seem a simple choice. Would he prefer to rise to his feet, take out a whip, and beat himself three thousand and three hundred times? Or, would he like to close his eyes and, bunching up his coat beneath his head, let the hand of slumber smooth his brow?

"When I'm asleep," the squire said (it seems he felt he must defend his choice), "I have no fears or hopes or toils or glory. Sleep is the cloak that covers human thought. It is the food that takes away our hunger. It is the water that takes away our thirst, the fire that warms the cold, the cold that chills the heat. It makes the shepherd equal to the king and makes the moron the equal to the sage."

But sleep would not descend on Sancho Panza, even if his master had allowed it.

From somewhere in the dark, and out of sight, there was a distant rumble coming closer.

Don Quixote stood and took his sword. Sancho rose as well, and then crouched down to hide beneath his donkey. What was this tumult, growing ever louder by the moment? It was a sound they'd heard before – something like the sound of charging bulls.

But it was not a pack of running bulls. This time it was a herd of pigs stampeding, grunting, snorting. Six hundred pigs driven to the local fair for selling.

Six hundred pigs sent our heroes sprawling in the dirt.

Six hundred pigs, they hurtled past to market, great pink beasts in such a fevered hurry. Let's not stop to think about their fates. Had they known what was in store, they'd surely have been hurtling the other way.

Don Quixote and his squire gathered their belongings, dusted off the road from their poor persons, helped their broken horse and ass to rise, and took the road anew – not knowing what the future had in store. They hurried on like innocent and luckless speeding pigs, as do we all.

The Beating Begins;
Don Alvaro Tarfe; Home at Last:
Where is Dulcinea?

༄

H omeward. On and on. The two were waylaid for a time by ruses cooked up by the duke and duchess. They caught wind that Quixote would be passing by, kidnapped him and Sancho, and staged another false extravaganza. But let us move along to matters much more pressing than the hollow entertainments of this twosome. Dulcinea's not been disenchanted.

༄

When would Sancho Panza tan his hide?

As our heroes traveled through the forest, Don Quixote gave the problem further thought. What could he do to spur his squire to action?

Finally a light went on in Don Quixote's desiccated brain. How had he not come up with this before?

"I worry," said Quixote to his squire, "that what I will suggest might somehow jinx my lady's disenchantment, but perhaps you would take money for your lashings? Why don't you look inside our purse and take from it whatever I can pay you."

Well, miracle of miracles, this time Sancho Panza was all ears. If he must give himself three thousand and three hundred lashes, fairness really did demand he end the task with something more than stinging welts.

"I'd happily subject myself to lashings," said the squire, "if there were something in it for myself. And by the way," he said, "if I seem greedy, I take this money for my wife and children."

"Oh, blessed Sancho Panza," said the knight. "Oh, kindly squire. My Lady Fair and I will be in your debt for as long as we abide here on this earth. If you were paid what you were owed for this, all the treasures stored in Venice would be yours."

Lashings must be done at night, it seems. That day dragged on and on for Don Quixote, so anxious was he that the lashings start. It was as if the sun stood still above them. Finally, night fell. With dinner done, Sancho made a whip from Dapple's reins.

He made his way into a stand of beech trees. He raised the lash and lowered down his breeches, brought down the reigns upon his naked flesh. Once. And then a second time. And it was on this second strike the squire knew that he was underpaid.

He called this out from in the stand of trees.

"Then double what I'll pay you," Quixote answered back.

"God's will be done," said Sancho. Sancho raised the lash and carried on.

But if the double payment did make Sancho's punishment more worth his while, he came up with a further means of ridding the ordeal of its worst aspects. Sancho turned his whip upon the trees. Groaning with each cracking of the whip, seeming to be suffering with every stroke, Sancho sighed as each blow met its mark. Quixote listened in the dark, counting up the lashes with his rosary. On and on the beating went, until Quixote, quailing at his squire's false distress (and worried, for his own sake, that his friend might die before he'd done his beating), called out:

"Sancho! Let this be enough for now!"

With one thousand lashes now accomplished, Sancho cried that he would carry on. On and on, he beat the trees, stripped them of their very bark. Finally, the knight came through the wood to stop him

Not seeing, or not choosing to, that Sancho Panza's flesh was still unbroken (and that the trees were rather worse for wear), Quixote wrapped his cloak around his squire and put his arms around his friend to comfort him. Sancho lay down on the ground to rest. He slept until the sun came up to warm him.

The next day, ten miles farther down the road, Don Quixote and Sancho Panza came upon an inn – the final inn they'll visit on their journey. Once again, Quixote saw the inn for what it was. He did not see a castle. He saw no moat, no drawbridge, and no towers. Had he regained his senses with defeat?

At the inn, Sancho Panza told the knight he would complete his punishment that night.

"No," said Don Quixote, "why don't you wait until we're home? We'll be home in La Mancha in two days."

"Why wait?" said Sancho Panza. "In delay lies danger. God helps those," he said, "who help themselves."

The two would wait for nightfall for the beating. But the empty afternoon before them would offer more than merely rest and food. A traveler arrived. The traveler had servants, one of whom, stopping for a moment at the entryway, addressed his master thus: "This inn seems clean and cool, Don Alvaro Tarfe. You can rest here."

Don Quixote started. "I know that name," he said to Sancho Panza. "I came upon it in the book of lies; the book that claims to be a second book recounting my adventures." (The book he had not dignified by reading.)

And Don Quixote's recollection was correct. The traveler who'd just arrived was indeed a person from the false account. As Don Quixote and his squire watched, the gentleman retired to his room.

Later in the afternoon, on a covered porch, Don Quixote, Sancho Panza, and the traveler met face-to-face.

Don Alvaro Tarfe spoke up first. He was, from all appearances, a pleasant sort.

"Where are you going, my dear sirs?" he asked of Don Quixote and the squire.

"To my village, which is nearby," said Quixote. And then he asked, "May I please know your name?"

"Don Alvaro Tarfe."

"By any chance, are you the fellow who appears in the Second Part of *The Ingenious Gentleman Don Quixote of La Mancha*, published by an author who is a liar, and has no gift for writing in the least?"

"I am." So said the traveler. "I knew Quixote very well. Indeed, I am the very man who, when the knight was sick and frail at home in bed, encouraged him to go back to his journeys. I took him all the way to Saragossa. In fact, I did him multitudes of favors and on one occasion, even saved his life. His fate was very sad, I'm sad to say. He is locked up in a madhouse in Toledo."

Don Quixote listened to these lies that in a former time

would have had him reaching for his sword. He somehow found forbearance to stay calm.

"And was this Don Quixote," asked the knight, "anything like me in his appearance? Did your Quixote resemble me at all?"

"Well, no. Not in the least," the stranger answered.

"And did he have a squire, Sancho Panza?"

"He did," Don Tarfe said. "But I'll confide his squire had nothing of the charm one had heard tell of. He was always straining to be funny, but he never was."

Not funny? Now Sancho Panza could not hold back. A man can only tolerate so much!

"This Sancho Panza, he was an imposter," said Sancho. "I am Sancho Panza and I am so funny that it's as though the sky has opened and rained down fun upon my very head. Fun pours forth from me at every turn. You'd know this if we spent some time together. Everyone around me laughs, even when I don't know why they're laughing. People say my jokes will be the death of them. That is how hilarious I am! And before you, sir, is Don Quixote, famous, wise and valorous, lover and righter of wrongs, and protector of widows and orphans, the slaughterer of maidens (Sancho likely said this by mistake), the knight whose Lady Fair is Dulcinea."

Sometimes people tell us things that have the ring of truth. We trust them by some instinct. And so it was that

Don Alvaro Tarfe knew the knight before him was Quixote.

"I believe you," said the traveler to Sancho. "I don't know why this is, but I believe you."

"I am Don Quixote," said Quixote, "and as it is quite clear you are a gentleman, I wonder if you'd grant me one small favor. Would you pay a visit to the mayor, so you might sign a formal declaration? It will state that you and I have never met before, and I am not the character that you were wrongly told was Don Quixote (the false Quixote of the False Part II)."

Don Tarfe agreed and — and then by sheer coincidence — the mayor happened through the inn's front door. Quixote wrote a statement, remembering to decorate the sentences with all the baffling terms and fancy phrases necessary to important papers — special outfits, if you will, to dress them up.

The document was signed and sealed. Quixote and his squire were on their way.

When darkness fell, the squire made his way into a lonely wood. He beat himself by way of beating trees until, at break of dawn, the count of lashes amounted to three thousand and two hundred twenty-nine.

One lash to go. On the night that followed, Sancho Panza gave a tree his final stroke. The sun would rise upon a world set straight.

On the morning after, Quixote woke, aware that on this happy day the curse upon his lady had been lifted. The sun that rose to shine on him rose as well to shine on Dulcinea, beautiful again to eye and nose. She was out there in the early Spanish dawn. Out there somewhere in the Spanish morning. Somewhere. She was somewhere. But, where *was* she?

All that day, Don Quixote and his squire stopped each maiden that the two encountered. Was this one Dulcinea? Or was this? Don Quixote trusted that the promise made by Merlin would be kept.

On they traveled, on and on, until at last, Don Quixote and his squire climbed a final hill. And at its crest they saw below, the landscape that had been their goal for all these miles. There, beneath them, lay their little village.

"Open up your eyes," called Sancho Panza, to the town below. "Beloved home! Look up! Behold! Here is your son, your Sancho Panza, if not rich, at least well whipped. Welcome, too, your great son, Don Quixote, conquered by another, but also conquered by himself. The finest kind of victory a man can have."

"Stop your nonsense," said the knight to Sancho. "Soon we will make plans for our new life."

But Dulcinea. Where was Dulcinea? So wondered Don Quixote in his heart of hearts.

࿇

Perhaps the truth would be revealed by signs. Benengeli tells us as our heroes came toward the village, they passed close by a threshing floor – a place where grain is shaken from the stems of plants. They heard two voices from behind a wall; little boys were arguing. One voice called out, insisting: "This will never happen."

This will never happen. Don Quixote heard these words. The blood within Quixote's veins turned cold.

"Did you hear the boy?" Quixote asked the squire. "Perhaps those words referred to my predicament. This means I'll not again see Dulcinea."

This will never happen.

Quixote was not one to miss an omen.

And lo! There was another sign (at least to Don Quixote's watchful eye). A rabbit now bore tidings of the future. A rabbit shot into the path, running from the teeth of chasing greyhounds, followed close by yelling, running men.

The rabbit ducked into our group and hid beneath the donkey's legs.

"A bad sign! Oh, a bad, bad sign!" Quixote cried. "Rabbits flee. Dogs chase. And Dulcinea does not come!"

Rabbits? Dogs? And Ladies Fair? Their fates were somehow magically combined? It was a subtle forecast to be sure.

"How can that be a bad sign?" asked the squire, taking up the rabbit in his arms. "You could just as easily imagine that this rabbit is the Lady Dulcinea. It's Dulcinea who scurries up to ask for your protection. Dulcinea who is safe and sound. Then it is a good sign, is it not?"

Sancho Panza placed the frightened creature in Quixote's arms, and as he did, the squabbling boys came out to show themselves. Why had they been fighting, asked the squire. One of them had said that there was something that would never ever happen. What did this mean?

The boy, whose voice they'd heard, spoke up. "I have his cricket cage. I was insisting I will never give it back — that this will never happen. And it won't."

Sancho Panza gave the boy some coins. Sancho bought the cricket cage and gave it to his master as a gift.

∽

At the outskirts of the town, the barber and the priest were the first to see our heroes had returned. They ran to Don Quixote and embraced him. Little boys ran off the spread the news.

At Don Quixote's household, his housekeeper and niece, teary-eyed with joy at his return, awaited their master on the stoop. And rushing down the road to Sancho Panza was his wife, holding their Sanchica by the hand. Untidy and half-dressed, Teresa had been caught off-guard. She could not help but notice (and she said so) that Sancho looked nothing like a governor.

"Let's go home and you shall hear some marvels," Sancho told her. "I've brought some money back. That's what counts. And I earned it without doing any harm."

"Good husband," said Teresa, "as long as you've brought money, I am happy. And whatever way you got it, I'm sure it's something that's been done before."

Sanchica hugged her father. She'd missed him, so she said, like rain when there is drought.

They turned for home, Sancho Panza and his wife and ass and daughter. Sancho led the donkey by the reins. Teresa held on to her husband's hand. Sanchica held her father by the belt loop. The four went down the village road tethered thus: by hands, by reins, by belt loops, and by love.

*

But, where was Dulcinea? Where was Dulcinea del Toboso? A cricket cage. A running bunny rabbit. Silence from the universe for now.

*

Before Quixote was inside his door, he'd told his house-keeper, his niece, the Bachelor, and priest of the plans that he'd come up with for their future. For one full year, he said, he'd be a shepherd, with Sancho and the Bachelor and priest. Don Quixote would invest in sheep. And while there were still details to be ironed out, the most essential task had been accomplished. Don Quixote had come up with names.

The Bachelor joined in with fresh ideas. "We will give our shepherdesses names that we will find in storybooks. Phyllis or Diana, Amaryllis, Florinda, Galatea, Belisandra. We'll carve these pretty names on every tree."

"Most fitting," said Quixote. "Although I have a shepherdess already – the peerless Dulcinea del Toboso, the glory of the riverbanks, the ornament of fields, the cream of grace, the focus of all praise, however overblown that praise might be!"

Overblown? The beauties of that shepherdess? Did Quixote know what he had said? And where was Dulcinea? Had the lady not been disenchanted?

To the priest and Bachelor, this plan (or so they said) was very sensible. This left it to the ladies to come out with the unromantic truth.

"Uncle," said the niece. "Just when we were hoping you were home for good! You want to go off into other mazes? Uncle! The straw is just too old for making whistles." (By which she meant that he was much too old.)

His housekeeper agreed. "You are too old to stand up to the heat of summer days, the cold of nights, the howling of the wolves who'd want your sheep. It is a life for men who have been raised to it, men who are much stronger than yourself." (By which she meant that he was frail, as well.)

"Hush," said Don Quixote. "I know best what I should do. Rest assured – if this is your concern – whatever my endeavors in this life, I will provide for you. Please take me to my bed. I feel unwell."

Of course, we know the housekeeper and niece were worried for our hero, not themselves. Quixote could be harsh, as we have seen. In any case, they took their master to his bed, and there he stayed.

His niece and his housekeeper – unromantic, maybe, but devoted – gave over every minute to his comfort, so glad were they to have their master home.

Our Story Ends

L ife doesn't last forever. True for speeding pigs and colored birds. True for running bunnies and for bandits. True for shepherds and for modest, lively ladies. True for Don Quixote, you, and me.

A fever came upon the knight. He lay in bed – no more a knight and not become a shepherd. His friends tried everything to cheer him. Sancho Panza did not leave his side.

Trying every means to lift his spirits, the Bachelor reported he'd purchased two fine dogs to watch their sheep. He'd come up with their names: Barcino and Butron. What's more, he had embarked upon some verse! Soon they would be world renowned as poets. Would Don Quixote rise up from his bed?

The doctor came. He listened to Quixote's pulse. "It is in truth a sadness that aflicts him. And sadness can be dangerous, indeed. He is in gravest danger. We should attend to the welfare of his soul."

Quixote listened calmly, but at his bedside his house-keeper and niece and Sancho Panza filled the room with tears.

The doctor left. Sancho left. Don Quixote slept for many hours – so many hours, the women were afraid he would not wake.

But Don Quixote did wake up, and when he did, they witnessed that a miracle had taken place. Don Quixote was a man much changed.

"Blessed is Almighty God." Quixote cried. "His mercy knows no limits."

"What are you saying, Uncle?" asked his niece. "What mercy does he show you, darling Uncle?"

"He has restored my mind to me," her master said. "My terrible delusions are cast off. My judgment is now clear, at last. I am awakened from the ignorance that came to me from reading books. Finally, at this late hour, I am restored to sanity. I tell you this, dear Niece, because I know I am about to die. Please call my friends. I must make my confession and my will."

Oh, if it was a miracle, why was it not the sort to save his life?

There was no need to call Quixote's friends. The priest, the barber, and the Bachelor were close at hand.

"Congratulate me," said the knight, "for I am no longer Don Quixote. I am the *hidalgo* who I was before. I am Alonso Quixano, who answered also to Alonso the Good. I am now an enemy of knights. And I abominate the books that drove me mad."

To Don Quixote's friends, exchanging anxious looks across his bed, this seemed a brand-new special sort of madness – to hate too much that thing that one has loved.

"What a thing to say!" replied the Bachelor. "To turn your back on everything you've done. Just when news has come that Lady Dulcinea's disenchanted. Have you not heard? She is restored! Dear friend, we, all of us, are going to be shepherds. We'll live like lords together in the fields."

"Please," said Don Quixote, "leave jests aside. At a time like this a man must not play games. These are my final hours on the earth. I must confess my sins and make a will."

All left the room except the priest, who made a list of Don Quixote's sins.

When confessions were complete, the priest came out of Don Quixote's room.

"The gentleman is sane and he is dying," said the priest. "And we must all go in and hear his will."

Sancho, who had stepped away a moment, hurried back to Don Quixote's bedside.

A notary, the housekeeper, the niece, the priest, the Bachelor, and Sancho Panza crowded into Don Quixote's room. (Quixote. You'll notice we still call him this; it's much too late to think of him by other names.)

"Don't die!" wept Sancho Panza. "Please don't die."

There was no silent crying now, but sobbing. Sobbing, faces wet with grief – the sort of loud untidy sorrow – the blubbering and slobbering, the crying out, and open sloppy suffering the good deserve.

"Don't die," cried Sancho Panza. "The maddest thing a man can do is die of grief, to let go of life for no good cause. You have not been knocked upon the head or stabbed. Get up out of bed. Let's all go off and live the life of shepherds. Perhaps we will encounter Dulcinea! We will find her, lovely as the dawn. She waits for you behind a hedge.

"And if you have a wish to die because you were defeated in a duel, blame me. I didn't take the proper pains to gird your horse. And knights are knocked off horses night and day. The knight who is defeated on one afternoon might find himself victorious the next."

"No use," said Don Quixote. "You won't find this year's birds in last year's nests."

⚬▨▨▨⚬

Don Quixote spoke his will aloud – housekeeping, to tidy up the bits and pieces of his life before he would move out and shut the door.

Money for the squire. Something for his housekeeper.

His properties were given to his niece, unless she was to marry someone with a taste for books of chivalry – the books that Don Quixote now despised. And Don Quixote finished off his will with this: "If my executors should meet the lying author of the Second Part of *The Ingenious Gentleman Don Quixote of La Mancha*, please beg him to forgive me for providing him with the opportunity to write the dreadful nonsense in his book."

Don Quixote fell into unconsciousness. There was a quiet ruckus in the room: hurrying and whispering, creased brows and wringing hands, creaking floorboards, rustling sheets, curtains drawn and water poured, and sobs held back and then released in gusts. For three days Don Quixote woke and fainted. And then he fainted for a final time. No trumpets and no cymbals and no horns.

A great event came creeping up and tapped him on the shoulder from behind.

For very often this is death, as though a soul has slipped out undetected, amid the clamor of clumsy human feelings.

It takes away the living from our midst and leaves an empty replica upon the bed.

Quixote's friends looked up and found him gone.

⟨◈⟩

The priest made a certificate. A notary was brought again. It had been Quixote's wish that there be a deed to prove his death. This proof that he had died would stay the wayward pens of lying authors. Only Benengeli would write the story of the knight Quixote.

⁊⁊⁊⁊⁊

But let us not forget the great Cervantes, who told us that he did not write this tale. He told us of a translator hired by a Mr. Benengeli. And Mr. Benengeli had pieced the tales together from fragments that he'd gathered here and there. And who had put those stories down on paper? Who was first?

We are not told. We never will be told, Cervantes wrote. Confusion on confusion in a maze.

⁊⁊⁊⁊⁊

The last words in the book are Benengeli's: "For me alone was Don Quixote born and I for him. It was for him to act, for me to write."

"Vale" he writes. It means "Be strong. Farewell."

⁊⁊⁊⁊⁊

And he is gone as well, like last year's clouds.